A COUNTESS
FOR CHRISTMAS

A COUNTESS FOR CHRISTMAS

BY

CHRISTY McKELLEN

First published in Great Britain 2016
By Mills & Boon, an imprint of HarperCollins*Publishers*
1 London Bridge Street, London, SE1 9GF

Large Print edition 2017

© 2016 Harlequin Books S.A.

Special thanks and acknowledgement are given to Christy McKellen for her contribution to the Maids Under the Mistletoe series.

ISBN: 978-0-263-07062-0

Printed and bound in Great Britain
by CPI Antony Rowe, Chippenham, Wiltshire

1119149080

This one's for all my wonderful friends,
especially Alice, Karen and Sophie,
my best buddies since our school days, and
for the fabulous ladies writing this continuity
with me, Kandy, Scarlet and Jessica,
who I'm also privileged to call my friends.

CHAPTER ONE

THIS HAD TO be the most challenging party that Emma Carmichael had ever worked at.

As fabulous as the setting was—a grand Chelsea town house that had been interior designed to within an inch of its life, presiding over the genteel glamour of Sloane Square—the party itself felt stilted and lifeless.

The trouble was, Emma mused as she glided inconspicuously through the throng, handing out drinks to the primped and polished partygoers, it was full of people who attended parties for a living rather than for pleasure, in an attempt to rub shoulders with London's great and good.

She knew all about that type of party after being invited to a glut of them in her late teens, either with her parents or with friends from her private girls' school in Cambridge. But she'd been a very different person then, pampered and carefree. Those privileged days were long gone now though, along with her darling late father's reputation and all their family's money.

As if her thoughts had conjured up the demons that had plagued her for the six years following his death, her phone vibrated in her pocket and she discreetly slipped it out and glanced at it, only to see it was another text message from her last remaining creditor reminding her she was late with her final repayment. Stomach sinking, she shoved the phone back into her pocket and desperately tried to reinstate the cheerful smile that her boss, Jolyon Fitzherbert, expected his staff to wear at all times.

'Emma, a word! Over here!' came the peremptory tones of the man himself from the other side of the room.

Darn. Busted.

Turning, she met her boss's narrowed eyes and swallowed hard as he beckoned her over to where he stood holding court to a small group of guests with one elbow propped jauntily against the vulgar marble fireplace.

Emma had encountered the bunch of repro-bates he was with a number of times since she'd begun working for Jolyon two months ago so she was well used to their contemptuous gazes that slid over her face as she approached now. They didn't believe in fraternising with the hired help.

If only Jolyon felt the same.

It was becoming harder and harder to avoid his wandering hands and suggestive gaze, es-pecially when she found herself alone with him. So far she'd been politely cool and it seemed to have held him at bay, but as soon as he got a couple of drinks into him dodging his advances became a whole lot harder.

Fighting down her apprehension, she gave Jolyon a respectful nod and smile as she came to a halt in front of him.

'Can I be of service?'

Jolyon's eyes seemed to bulge with men-ace in his flushed face. 'I do hope I didn't just see you playing with your mobile phone when you're supposed to be serving these good people, Emma, because that would be rude and unprofessional, would it not?' he drawled.

Emma's stomach rolled with unease. 'Er— yes. I mean no, I wasn't—' She could feel heat creeping up her neck as the whole group stared at her with ill-disguised disdain. 'I was just checking—'

'I'm sure you think you're too good to be serving drinks to the likes of us—' Jolyon said loudly over the top of her, layering his voice with haughty sarcasm.

'No, of course not—'

The expression on his face was now half leer, half snarl. '—but since I'm paying you to be here, I expect to have your full attention.'

'Yes, of course, Jolyon. You absolutely have it,' Emma said, somehow managing to dredge up a smile, despite the sickening pull of humiliation dragging her spirits down towards the floor.

He eyed her with an unnerving twinkle of

malice in his expression, as if he was getting a thrill out of embarrassing her. 'In that case I'll have a large whisky.'

Emma opened her mouth to ask whether anyone else in the group required anything, but before the words could emerge Jolyon flapped a dismissive hand in her face and barked, 'Go on, fetch!'

Stumbling backwards, stupefied by his rudeness, she gave him a jerky nod and turned away, mortification flooding her whole body with unwelcome heat.

Twisting the chain she always wore around her neck to remind her of better times—before everything in her life had gone to hell in a hand basket—she took a deep, calming breath as she walked stiffly over to where Jolyon kept his whisky decanter in an antique burr walnut drinks cabinet. Pouring his regular measure of two fingers of the dark amber liquid into a cut-glass tumbler with a shaking hand, she managed to slosh a little over the rim and had to surreptitiously wipe it off the wood with her apron so she didn't get shouted at for not treating his furniture with due respect.

That was the most frustrating thing about working for Jolyon; he treated *her* with less respect than an inanimate object and all she could do was bite her lip and get on with it.

Clio Caldwell, who ran the high-end agency Maids in Chelsea that had found her this housekeeping position, had warned her that Jolyon was a difficult character when she'd offered her the job, but since he also paid extremely well Emma had decided she was prepared to handle his irascible outbursts and overly tactile ways if she was well remunerated for it. If she could just stick it out here for a little while longer she'd be in the position to pay off the last of her father's debts and be able to put this whole sordid business to bed, then she could finally move on with her life.

What a relief that would be.

Out of nowhere the old familiar grief hit her hard in the chest.

Some days she missed her father so much her

heart throbbed with pain. What she wouldn't give to have him back again, enveloping her in a great big bear hug and telling her that everything was going to be okay, that she was loved and that he wouldn't let anything hurt her.

But she knew she was being naïve. All the years he'd been telling her that, he'd actually been racking up astronomical debts. The life that she'd once believed was real and safe had evaporated into thin air the moment she'd lost him to a sudden heart attack and her mother had promptly fallen apart, leaving her to deal with a world of grief and uncertainty on her own.

Gripping the tumbler so hard her knuckles cracked, she returned to where her boss stood. 'Here you go, Jolyon,' she said calmly.

He didn't even look at her, just took the glass from her outstretched hand and turned his back on her, murmuring something to the man next to him, who let out a low guffaw and gave Emma the most fleeting of glances.

It reminded her all too keenly of the time right after her father's funeral when she couldn't go anywhere without being gossiped about and stared at with a mixture of pity and condescension.

Forcing herself to ignore the old familiar sting of angry defensiveness, she plastered a nonchalant smile onto her face and dashed back to the kitchen, and sanctuary.

Stumbling in through the door, she let out a sigh of relief, taking a moment to survey the scene and to centre herself, feeling her heart rate begin to slow down now that she was back in friendly company.

She didn't want anyone in here to see how shaken up she was, not when she was supposed to be the one in charge of running the party. After years of handling difficult situations on her own she was damned if she was going to fall apart now.

Fortunately, Clio at the agency had come up trumps with the additional waiting staff for the party today. Two of the girls, Sophie and Grace, had become firm friends of hers after they'd all found themselves working at a lot of the same events throughout the last year. Before meeting these two it had been a long time since Emma had had friends that she could laugh with so easily. The very public scandal surrounding her father's enormous debts had put paid to a lot of what she'd thought were solid friendships in the past—owing someone's family an obscene amount of money would do that to a relationship, it seemed, especially within the censorious societal set in which she used to circulate.

Sophie, a bubbly blonde with a generous smile and a quick wit, had brought along an old school friend of hers tonight too, a cute-as-a-button Australian who was visiting England for a few months called Ashleigh, whose glossy mane of chestnut-red hair shone so radiantly under the glaring kitchen lights it was impossible to look away from her.

During short breaks in serving the partygoers that evening, the four of them had bonded while having a good giggle at some of the entitled behaviour they'd witnessed.

Emma's mirth had been somewhat tainted

though, by the memory of how she'd acted much the same way when she was younger and how ashamed she felt now about taking her formerly privileged life so much for granted.

'Hey, lovely ladies,' she said, joining them at the kitchen counter where they were all busying about, filling fresh glasses with pink champagne and mojitos for the demanding guests.

'Hey, Emma, I was just telling Ashleigh how much fun it was, working at the Snowflake Ball last New Year's Eve,' Sophie said, making her eyebrows dance with delight. 'Are you working there again this year? Please say yes!'

'I hope so, as long as Jolyon agrees to give me the time off. He's supposed to be going skiing in Banff, so I should be free for it,' Emma said, shooting her friend a hopeful smile.

The annual New Year's Snowflake Ball was a glittering and awe-inspiring event that the whole of Chelsea society turned out for. Last year she and the girls had enjoyed themselves immensely from the wings after serving the guests with the most delectable—and eye-wateringly expensive—food and drink that London had to offer. Caught up in the romance of it all, Emma had even allowed herself to fantasise along with the others about how perhaps they'd end up attending as guests one day, instead of as waiting staff.

Not that there was a snowflake's chance in hell of that happening any time soon, not with her finances in their current state.

'Are you ladies working there too?' Emma asked, bouncing her gaze from Sophie to Grace, then on to Ashleigh.

Grace, a willowy, strikingly pretty woman who wore a perpetual air of no-nonsense purpose like a warm but practical coat, flashed her a grin. 'Wouldn't miss it for the world. You should definitely let Clio know if you're interested, Ashleigh.' She turned to give the bright-eyed redhead an earnest look. 'I know she's looking for smart, dedicated people to work at that event. She'd snap you up in a second.'

'Yeah, I might. I'm supposed to be going back to Australia to spend Christmas with my folks, but I don't know if I can face it,' Ashleigh said, self-consciously smoothing a strand of hair behind her ear. 'It's not going to be much of a celebratory atmosphere if I'm constantly trying to avoid being in the same room as my ex-fiancé the whole time.'

'He's going to be at your parents' house for Christmas?' Grace asked, aghast. 'Wow. Awkward.'

'Yeah, just a bit,' Ashleigh said, shuffling on the spot. 'If I do stay here I'm going to have to find another place to live though. I'm only booked into the B and B until the beginning of December, which means I've got less than a month to find new digs.' She glanced at them all, her eyes wide with hope. 'Anyone looking for a roomie by any chance? I'll take a floor, a sofa, whatever you've got!'

'Sorry, sweetheart,' Sophie said, shaking her head so her long sleek hair swished across her shoulders. 'As you know, my tiny bedroom's barely big enough for the single mattress I have in it and with my living area doubling as my dressmaking studio I can't even see the sofa under all the boxes of cloth and sewing materials.' She smiled grimly. 'And even if I could, it's on its last legs and not exactly comfortable.'

The other girls shook their heads too.

'I can't help either, Ashleigh, I'm afraid,' Emma said. 'My mother's staying with me on and off at the minute while her place in France is being damp proofed and redecorated and I don't think her nerves would take having someone she doesn't know kipping on the sofa. She's a little highly strung like that.'

'No worries,' Ashleigh said, batting a hand even though her shoulders remained tense, 'I'm sure something will turn up.'

One of the other waitresses came banging into the kitchen then, looking harassed.

'Emma, the guests are starting to complain about running out of drinks out there.'

'On it,' Emma said, picking up a tray filled with the drinks that Grace had been diligently pouring throughout their conversation and backing out through the swinging kitchen door with it.

'Later, babes.'

Turning round to face the party, readying herself to put on her best and most professional smile again, her gaze alighted on a tall male figure that she'd not noticed before on the other side of the room. There was an intense familiarity about him that shot an unsettling feeling straight to her stomach.

It was something about the breadth of his back and the way his hair curled a little at his nape that set her senses on high alert. The perfect triangle of his body, which led her gaze down to long, long legs, was her idea of the perfect male body shape.

A shape she knew as well as her own and a body she'd once loved very, very much.

Blood began to pump wildly through her veins.

The shape and body of Jack Westwood, Earl of Redminster.

The man in question turned to speak to someone next to him, revealing his profile and confirming her instincts.

It was him.

Prickly heat cascaded over her skin as she stared with a mixture of shock and nervous excitement at the man she'd not set eyes on for six years.

Ever since her life had fallen apart around her.

Taking a step backwards, she looked wildly around her for some kind of cover to give her a moment to pull herself together, but other than dashing back to the kitchen, which she couldn't do without drawing attention to herself, there wasn't any.

What was he doing here? He was supposed to be living in the States heading up the billion-dollar global electronics empire he'd left England to set up six years ago.

At the age of twenty-one he'd been dead set on making a name for himself outside the aristocratic life he'd been born into and had been determined not to trade on the family name but to make a success of himself through hard work and being the best in his field. From what she'd read in the press it seemed he'd been very successful at it too. But then she'd always known he would be. The man positively exuded power and intelligence from every pore.

After reading in the papers that his grandfather had died recently she'd wondered whether he'd come back to England.

It looked as if she had her answer.

He was surrounded, as ever, by a gaggle of beautiful women, all looking at him as if he was the most desirable man on earth. It had always been that way with him; he drew women to him like bees to a honeypot. The first time she'd ever laid eyes on him, at the tender age of twelve, he'd been surrounded by girls desperate for his attention. His sister, Clare—her best friend from her exclusive day school—had laughed and rolled her eyes about it, but Emma knew she loved her brother deeply and was in awe of his charisma.

Emma, on the other hand, had spent years feeling rattled and annoyed by his unjustified judgemental sniping at her and for a long time she'd thought he truly disliked her. Her greatest frustration at that point in her life was not being able to work out why.

As she watched, still frozen to the spot, one of the women in his group leaned towards him, laying a possessive hand on his arm as she murmured something into his ear, and Emma's heart gave an extra-hard squeeze.

Was he with her?

The thought made her stomach roll with nausea.

Feeling as though she'd stepped into the middle of one of her nightmares, she took a tentative pace sideways, hoping to goodness he wouldn't choose that exact moment to turn around and see her standing there wearing her Maids in Chelsea apron, holding a tray of drinks.

'Hey, you, don't just stand there gawping, missy, bring me one of those drinks. I'm parched!' one of Jolyon's most obstreperous acquaintances shouted over to her.

Face flaming, Emma sidestepped towards

him, keeping Jack's broad back in her peripheral vision, hoping, *praying*, he wouldn't spot her.

Unfortunately, because she wasn't paying full attention to where she was stepping, she managed to stand on the toe of the woman talking with Mr Shouty, who then gave out a loud squeal of protest, flinging her arms out and catching the underside of the tray Emma was holding. Before she had a chance to save it, the entire tray filled with fine crystal glasses and their lurid contents flipped up into the air, then rained down onto the beige carpet that Jolyon had had laid only the week before.

Gaudy-coloured alcohol splattered the legs of the man standing nearby and a deathly silence fell, swiftly followed by a wave of amused chatter and tittering in its wake.

Emma dropped to her knees, desperately trying to save the fine crystal glasses from being trampled underfoot, feeling the sticky drinks that now coated the carpet soak into her skirt and tights.

All she needed now was for Jolyon to start shouting at her in front of Jack and her humiliation would be complete.

Glancing up through the sea of legs, desperate to catch the eye of a friendly face so she could escape quickly, her stomach flipped as her gaze connected with a pair of the most striking eyes she'd ever known.

Jack Westwood was staring at her, his brow creased into a deep frown and the expression on his face as shocked as she suspected hers had been to see him only moments ago.

Heart thumping, she tore her gaze away from his, somehow managing to pile the glasses haphazardly back onto the tray with shaking hands, then stand up and push her way through the agitated crowd, back to the safety of the kitchen.

'Sorry! Sorry!' she muttered as she shuffled past people. 'I'll be back in a moment to clean up the mess. Please mind your feet in case there's any broken glass.'

Her voice shook so much she wouldn't have

been surprised if nobody had understood a word she'd said.

Please let him think he just imagined it was me. Please, please!

As she stumbled into the kitchen the first person she saw was Grace.

'Oh, my goodness, Emma! What happened?'

Her friend darted towards her, relieving her of the drinks tray with its precariously balanced glasses.

Grabbing the worktop for support, Emma took a couple of deep breaths before turning to face her friend's worried expression.

'Emma? Are you okay? You're as white as a sheet,' Sophie gasped, also alerted by her dramatic entrance. 'Did someone say something to you? Did they hurt you?' From the mixture of fear and anger on Sophie's face, Emma suspected her friend had some experience in that domain.

'No, no, it's nothing like that.' She swallowed hard, desperately grasping for some semblance of cool, but all her carefully crafted control seemed to have deserted her the moment she'd spotted Jack.

'There's someone here—someone I haven't seen for a very long time,' she said, her voice wobbling with emotion.

He'd always had this effect on her, turning her brain to jelly and her heart to goo, and after six long years without hearing the deep rumble of his voice or catching sight of his breathtaking smile or breathing in his heady, utterly beguiling scent her body seemed to have gone into a frenzy of longing for him.

'I wasn't expecting to see him, that's all. It took me by surprise,' she finished, forcing a smile onto her face.

The girls didn't look convinced by her attempt at upbeat nonchalance, which wasn't surprising considering she was still visibly trembling.

'So when you say "him",' Ashleigh said, with a shrewd look in her eye, 'I'm guessing we're talking about an ex here?'

Emma nodded and looked away, not wanting to be drawn into giving them the painful details about what had happened between her and Jack. She needed to be able to do her job here tonight, or risk being fired, and if she talked about him now there was a good chance she'd lose her grip on her very last thread of calm.

'It's okay, I can handle it, but I managed to drop a whole tray of drinks out there. The carpet's absolutely covered in booze right by the camel-coloured sofa and I managed to spray the legs of a partygoer as well. He didn't seem entirely pleased to be showered in pink champagne.' She let out a shaky laugh.

'Don't worry, Emma, we'll cover it,' Grace said, putting a reassuring hand on her arm. 'Sophie, find a cloth to mop up as much of the liquid as possible, will you?'

'Will do,' Sophie said, swivelling on the spot and heading over to the broom cupboard where all the cleaning materials were kept.

'Ashleigh—'

'I'll get another tray of drinks out there right now and go and flirt with the guy you splattered with booze,' Ashleigh cut in with a smile, first at Emma, then at Grace.

'Great,' Grace said, grinning back. 'Emma, go and sit down with your head between your knees until your colour returns.'

'But—' Emma started to protest, but Grace put her hands on her shoulders and gently pushed her back towards one of the kitchen chairs.

Emma sat down gratefully, relieved that everything was being taken care of but experiencing a rush of embarrassment at causing so much trouble for her friends.

After a moment of sitting quietly, her heart rate had almost returned to normal and the feeling that she was about to pass out had receded.

She was just about to stand up and get back out there, determined not to shy away from this, but to deal with Jack's reappearance head-on, when Sophie came striding back into the kitchen.

'You look better,' she said, giving Emma an assessing once-over.

'Yeah, I'm okay now. Ready to get back out there.'

'You know, you could stay in the kitchen and orchestrate things from here if you want. We can handle keeping all the guests happy out there.'

Emma sighed, grateful to her friend for the offer, but knowing that hiding wasn't an option.

'Thanks, but I can't stay in here all evening. Jolyon expects me to be out there charming his guests and keeping a general eye on things.' Rubbing a hand over her forehead, she gave her friend a smile, which she hoped came across with more confidence than she felt.

'Okay, well, let's fix your hair a bit, then,' Sophie said, moving towards her with her hands outstretched. 'We'll get it out of that restricting band and you can use it to shield your face if you need to hide for a second.'

Grateful for her friend's concern, Emma let Sophie gently pull out the band that was holding her up-do neatly away from her face so that her long sheet of hair swung down to cover each side of her face.

'It's such a beautiful colour—baby blonde,' Sophie said appreciatively, her gaze sweeping from one side of Emma's face to the other. 'Is it natural?'

Emma nodded, feeling gratified warmth flood her cheeks. 'Yes, thank goodness. I'd never be able to afford the hairdressing bills.' Her thoughts flew back to how much money she used to waste on expensive haircuts in her pampered youth and she cringed as she considered what she could do with that money now— things like putting it towards the cost of more night classes and studying materials.

The kitchen door banged open, making them both jump, and Emma's gaze zeroed in on the puce-coloured face of Jolyon Fitzherbert as he advanced towards her.

'Emma! What's going on? Why are you skulking in here when you should be out there making sure my party's running smoothly? And what the hell was that, throwing a tray of drinks all over my new carpet?'

She put up a placating hand, realising her mistake when his scowl only deepened. Jolyon hated it when people tried to soothe him.

'I was just checking on the stores of alcohol in here. I'm going back out there right now,' she said, plastering a benevolent smile onto her face.

Jolyon's eyes narrowed. 'Come with me,' he ground out, turning clumsily on the spot and giving away just how drunk he was.

Sophie put a hand on Emma's arm, but she brushed her off gently. 'It's okay, I can handle him. You make sure everything runs smoothly here while I'm dealing with this, okay?' She gave her friend a beseeching look, pleading for her support, and was rewarded with a firm nod.

'No problem.'

Running to catch up with Jolyon, Emma saw him unlocking the door to his study and the lump in her throat thickened. This couldn't be good. She was only ever summoned to his study when he felt something had gone badly wrong. He liked to sit behind his big oak desk in his puffy leather armchair as if he were lord of the manor and she were his serving wench being given a severe dressing-down.

Deciding to pre-empt his lecture, she put out both hands in a gesture of apology. 'Jolyon, I'm very sorry about dropping those drinks. It was a genuine accident and I promise it won't ever happen again.'

Stopping before he reached the desk, he turned to regard her through red-rimmed eyes, his gaze a little unfocussed due to the enormous amount of whisky he'd drunk throughout the evening.

'What are you going to do to make it up to me?' he asked.

She didn't like the expression in his eyes. Not one little bit.

'I'll pay to have the carpet professionally cleaned. None of the glasses broke, so it's just the stain that needs taking care of.'

He shook his head slowly. 'I don't think that's apology enough. You ruined my party!'

Despite knowing it would be unwise to push him when he was in this kind of mood, she couldn't help but fold her arms and tilt up her chin in defiance. She might have made a bit of a mess, but, if anything, her little accident had livened the party up.

'Jolyon, everyone's having a great time. You've thrown a wonderful party here today,' she said carefully. What she actually wanted to do was suggest where he could shove his job, but she bit her lip, mentally picturing the meagre numbers in her bank balance rapidly ticking down if she let her anger get the better of her.

As she'd predicted, her boldness only seemed to exacerbate his determination to have his pound of flesh and he took a deliberate step towards her and, lifting his hand, he slid it roughly under her jaw and into her hair. His grip was decisive and strong and she acknowledged a twinge of unease in the pit of her stomach as she realised how alone they were in here, away from the rest of the party.

He began to stroke his thumb along her jaw,

grazing the bottom of her lip. Waves of revulsion flooded through her at his touch, but she didn't move. She needed to brazen this out. She knew exactly what he was like—if you showed any sign of weakness that was it, you were fired on the spot.

'Well, you ruined it for me,' he growled, moving even closer so she could smell the sharp tang of whisky on his breath. 'But perhaps we can figure out a satisfactory way for you to make it up to me,' he said, his gaze roving lasciviously over her face and halting on her mouth.

She clamped her lips together, racking her brains for a way out of this without making the situation worse.

'Jolyon, let go of me,' she said, forcing as much authority into her voice as she could summon, which wasn't a lot. 'I need to get back to the party and serve your guests and they'll be missing you, wondering where you are,' she said, grasping for something—anything—to aid her getaway. Appealing to his ego had worked well before, but she could tell from the look in

his eyes that it wasn't going to fly this time.
He wanted much more than a verbal apology
from her.

The thought made her shudder.

Taking a sudden step backwards, she managed to break his hold on her. 'I need to get
back. Let's talk about this tomorrow, shall we?'
Before he could react, she turned and walked
swiftly out of the door and back towards the
noisy hubbub of the party, her heart thumping
hard against her ribcage and the erratic pulse
of her blood spurring her on.

She heard him come after her, his breath rasp-
ing in his throat as his movements picked up
into a drunken jog. She'd just made it to the
living-room doorway when he caught up with
her, grabbing hold of her arm and spinning her
around to face him.

'Jolyon, please—' she gasped, then froze in
horror as his lips came crashing down onto hers,
his arms wrapping around her like a vice. She
couldn't breathe, couldn't move, her heart ham-

mering hard in her ears as she struggled to get away from him—

Then suddenly he seemed to let go of her— or was he being dragged away? The loud *ooof!* sound he made in the back of his throat made her think that perhaps he *had* been and she spun around only to come face to face with Jack.

His mesmerising eyes bore into hers, blazing with anger as a muscle ticced in his clenched jaw, and her stomach did a slow somersault. His gaze swept over her face for the merest of seconds before moving to lock onto Jolyon instead, who was now leaning against the doorjamb, gasping as if he'd been winded.

'What do you want, Westwood?' Jolyon snapped at Jack, flashing him a look of fear-tinged contempt.

Jack glared back, his whole body radiating tension as if he was having to physically restrain himself from landing a punch right on Jolyon's pudgy jaw.

He took a purposeful step towards the cow-ering man and leaned one strong arm on the jamb above Jolyon's head, forming a formidable six-foot-three enclosure of angry, powerful man around him.

'I want you to keep your hands off my wife!'

CHAPTER TWO

JACK WESTWOOD KNEW he'd made a monumental mistake the moment he heard the collective gasp of the crowd in the room behind him.

What the hell had he just done?

It wasn't like him to lose his head, in fact he was famous in the business circles in which he presided for being a cool customer and impossible to intimidate, but seeing Emma again like this had shaken him to his very soul.

It occurred to him with a sick twist of irony that the last time he'd acted so rashly was when he'd asked her to marry him. She'd always had this effect on him, messing with his head and undermining his control until he didn't know which way was up.

Logically he knew he should have stayed away from her tonight, just until he was men-

tally prepared to see her again, but after finding
he couldn't concentrate on a word anyone had
said to him after he'd spotted her earlier his instinct had been to search her out, then jump in
to defend her when he'd seen Fitzherbert trying to kiss her.

She was still his wife after all, even if they
hadn't had any contact for the last few years—
that was what had prompted him to do it. That
and the fact he hated any kind of violence towards women.

The searing anger he'd felt at seeing this idiot
being so rough with her still buzzed through
his veins. Who did he think he was, forcing
himself on a woman who clearly wasn't interested in him? And it was obvious that Emma
wasn't. He knew her too well not to be able to
read her body language and interpret her facial
expressions, even when she was trying to hide
her true feelings.

'Emma, are you okay?' he asked, turning to
check her face for bruises. But it seemed all
that was bruised was her pride. At least that

was what the flash of discomfiture in her eyes led him to believe.

'I'm fine, thank you, Jack. I can handle this,' she said, laying a gentle hand on his arm and giving him a supplicatory smile.

Unnerved by the prickle of sensation that rushed across his skin where she touched him, he shook the feeling off, putting it down to his shock at seeing her again mixed in with the tension of the situation. Nodding, he took a couple of steps backwards, allowing Jolyon to push himself upright, and watched with bitter distaste as the man brushed himself down with shaking hands and rolled back his portly shoulders.

'I'd like you both to leave,' Fitzherbert said, his voice firm, even if it did resonate with a top note of panic.

Jack turned to see Emma looking at Fitzherbert with a pleading expression, making him think that leaving was the last thing she wanted to do. Why on earth would she want to stay? Unless they were together as a couple?

The thought of that made him shudder. Surely

she couldn't have stooped so low as to have attached herself to a playboy like Fitzherbert. He knew she'd been brought up living the high life, was used to being taken care of by other people, but this was beyond the pale.

'Jolyon, please, this is just a misunderstanding. Can we talk about it—?'

Fitzherbert held up a hand to halt her speech and shook his head slowly, his piggy eyes squinty and mean.

'I don't want to hear it, Emma. I want you to leave. Right now. The other girls can cover for you. From what I've seen tonight that's already been happening anyway. Whenever I've looked for you, you've been skulking in the kitchen.'

'I've been orchestrating the party from there, Jolyon—'

He held up his hand higher, his palm only inches away from her face.

Jack experienced a low throb of anger at the condescension of the act, but he kept his mouth shut. He didn't think Emma would appreciate him butting in right now. He'd let her handle this.

For now.

'Didn't you hear me, Emma? You're fired!' There was no mistaking Fitzherbert's tone now. Even though he was drunk, his conviction was clear.

Fired? So she was working for him? Jack found this revelation even more shocking than the idea that they'd been a couple.

She went to argue, but Fitzherbert shouted over her.

'I specifically requested the agency find me a housekeeper that wasn't married so there wouldn't be any difficulties with priorities. I need someone who can work late into the evening or on short notice without having to check with a partner first. I've been burned by problems like that before.'

He glanced at Jack now, his expression full of reproach. 'A *decent* chap doesn't want his *wife* working for a bachelor such as myself.'

By that, Jack assumed what Fitzherbert actually meant was that he'd wanted the option to pursue more than just housekeeping duties with his employees without the fear of a husband turning up to spoil his fun, or, worse, send him to the hospital.

A prickle of pure disgust shot up his spine at the thought.

'You said in your application that you were unmarried,' Fitzherbert went on, apparently choosing to ignore Jack's balled fists and tense stance now.

'You lied. So I'm terminating our contract forthwith. I don't want a liar as well as the daughter of a wastrel working in my house.'

Shock clouded Emma's face at this low jibe and Fitzherbert smiled and leaned closer to her, clearly relishing the fact that he'd hit a nerve. 'Yes, that's right, I know all about your father's reputation for spending other people's money. I make sure to look up everyone I employ in order to protect myself.'

He jabbed a finger at her. 'I gave you the benefit of the doubt because you're a hard worker and easy on the eye...' his snarl increased '...but who knows what could have gone missing in the time you've been here?'

That did it.

'Don't you dare speak to her like that!' Jack ground out.

Emma turned to him with frustration in her eyes and held up a hand. 'Jack, I said I can handle this. Please keep out of it!'

'No wonder you've kept your marriage to her a secret if that's the way she speaks to you,' Fitzherbert muttered, slanting Jack a sly glance.

'Oh, go to hell, Jolyon,' Emma shot back, with a vehemence that both surprised and impressed Jack. 'You know what, you can keep your measly job. I was going to leave at the end of the month anyway. Your wandering hands had got a bit too adventurous for my liking.'

And with that, she pulled an apron that Jack had not noticed she was wearing before from around her middle and dropped it on the floor at Fitzherbert's feet, then spun on her heel and strode towards the front door.

Glancing back into the room, Jack saw that a large crowd of partygoers had gathered to watch their tawdry little show and every one of them was now staring at him in curious anticipation.

It suddenly occurred to him that they were waiting for him to chase after his *wife*.

Damn it.

Now the secret was out, he was going to have to find a way to handle this situation without causing more problems for himself. The last thing he needed was to catch the attention of the gutter press when he was just finding his feet again here in England. Knowing Emma as he did, he was aware that it would be down to him to handle the fallout from this, which was fine, he was used to dealing with complex situations in his role as CEO so this shouldn't be much of a stretch, but he could really do without an added complication like this right now.

Throwing Fitzherbert one last disgusted

glance, Jack turned his back on the man then went to grab his overcoat from the peg by the door. Following Emma out, he caught her up as she exited into the cold mid-November night air.

She didn't turn round as she hopped down the marble steps of the town house and out into the square.

'Emma, wait!' Jack shouted, worried she might jump into a cab and he'd lose her before he had a chance to figure out what he was going to do about all this.

'Why did you have to get involved, Jack?' she asked, swinging round to face him, her cheeks pink and her eyes wild with a mixture of embarrassment and anxiety.

The sight of it stopped him in his tracks. Even in his state of agitation he was acutely aware that she was still a heart-stoppingly beautiful woman. If anything she was even more beautiful now than when he'd last seen her six years ago, with those full wide lips that used to haunt his dreams and those bright, intelligent green eyes that had always glowed with spirit and an innate joy of life.

Not that she looked particularly joyful right now.

Shaking off the unwelcome rush of feelings this brought, he folded his arms and raised an eyebrow at her.

'I wasn't going to just stand by and watch Fitzherbert manhandle you like that,' he said, aiming for a cool, reasonable tone. There was no way he was going to have a public row in the middle of Sloane Square with her. What if there were paparazzi lurking behind one of the trees nearby?

He shifted on the spot. 'I would have done the same for any woman in that position.'

There was a flash of hurt in her eyes. 'Well, for future reference, I can take care of myself, thanks. It wasn't your place to get involved, Jack.'

The muscles in his shoulders tensed instinctively. 'I'm your husband. Of course it was my place.'

She sighed, kicking awkwardly at the ground. 'Technically, maybe, but nobody knew that. I certainly haven't told anyone.'

He was annoyed by how riled he felt by her saying that, as if he was a dirty secret she'd been keeping.

It was on the tip of his tongue to start demanding answers of her—about what had happened in the intervening years to make it necessary for her to work for a man like Fitzherbert and why she hadn't contacted him once in the six years they'd been estranged, even just to let him know that she was okay.

But he didn't, because this wasn't the time or place to discuss things like that.

'Why did you shout about us being married in front of all those people?' she asked, her voice wobbling a little now.

He took a deep breath, rubbing a hand over his forehead in agitation. 'I reacted without thinking in the heat of the moment.'

That had always been his problem when she was around. For some reason she shook him up, made him lose control, like no one else in the world could.

To his surprise the corner of her mouth quirked into a reluctant smile. 'Well, it's going to be round Chelsea society like wildfire now. That crowd loves a bit of salacious gossip.'

Sighing, he batted a hand at her. 'Don't worry, people will talk for a while, then it'll become old news. I'll handle it.'

She looked at him for a moment, her eyes searching his face as if checking for reassurance.

Jack stared back at her, trying not to let a sudden feeling of edginess get to him. As much as he'd love to be able to brush the problem of them still being married under the carpet he knew it would be a foolish thing to do. There was no point in letting it drag on any more now he was back. It needed to be faced head-on so they could resolve it quickly and with as little pain as possible.

Because, inevitably, it would still be painful for them, even after all this time.

Emma tore her gaze away from him, frowning down at the pavement now and letting out a growl of frustration. 'I could have done with keeping that job. It paid really well,' she muttered. 'And who knows what the knock-on effect of embarrassing Jolyon like that is going to be?'

He balled his fists, trying to keep a resurgence of temper under control at the memory of Fitzherbert's treatment of her. 'He won't do anything—the man's a coward.'

'Jolyon's an influential man around here,' she pointed out, biting her lip. 'He has the ear of a lot of powerful people.'

She stared off into the distance, her breath coming rapidly now, streaking the dark night air with clouds of white. 'Hopefully Clio at the agency will believe my side of the story and still put me forward for other jobs, but people might not want to take me on if Jolyon gets to them first.'

'Surely you don't need a job that badly?' he asked, completely bemused by her anxiety about not being able to land another waitressing role. What had happened to her plans to go to university? She couldn't have been working in the service industry all this time, could she?

The rueful smile she flashed him made something twang in his chest.

'Unfortunately I do, Jack. We can't all be CEO of our own company,' she said with a teasing glint in her eye now.

He huffed out a mirthless laugh and shook his head, recalling how it had been through Emma's encouragement that he'd accepted the prodigious offer for a highly sought-after job at an electronics company in the States right after graduating from university, which had enabled him to chase his dream of setting up his own company.

It had been an incredible opportunity and one he'd been required to act on quickly. Emma had understood how important it had been to him to become financially independent on his own merits, rather than trading on his family name as his father had, and had urged him to go. In a burst of youthful optimism, he'd asked her to marry him so she could go with him. She'd been all he could think about when he was twenty-one. He'd been obsessed with her—every second away from her had felt empty—and the mere suggestion of leaving her behind in England had filled him with dismay.

In retrospect it had been ridiculous for them to tie the knot so young; with him only just graduated from Cambridge University and she only eighteen years old.

They'd practically been children then: closeted and naïve.

She coughed and took an awkward step backwards and he realised with a start that he'd been scowling at her while these unsettling memories had flitted through his mind.

'It's good to see you again, Jack, despite the less than ideal circumstances,' she said softly, her expression guarded and her voice holding a slight tremor now, 'but I guess I should get going.'

She seemed to fold in on herself and he realised with a jolt that she was shivering.

'Where's your coat?' he asked, perhaps a little more sharply than was necessary.

'It's back in the house, along with my handbag,' she muttered. 'I can't go back in there for them now though. I'll give one of the girls a ring when I get home and ask her to drop them over to me tomorrow.' She paused as a sheepish look crossed her face. 'I don't suppose you could lend me a couple of pounds for my bus fare, could you?'

The tension in her voice touched something deep inside him, making him suddenly conscious of what a rough night she was having.

'Yes, of course.' Taking off his overcoat, he wrapped it around her shoulders. 'Here, take my coat. There's money in the pocket.'

She looked up at him with wide, grateful eyes. 'Are you sure?'

'Yes,' he clipped out, a little unnerved by how his body was responding to the way she was looking at him.

He cleared his throat. 'Will you be able to get into your—er—flat?' he asked. He wasn't sure where she was living now. He'd heard that she'd moved to London after they'd sold the family home in Cambridge, but other than that his information about her was a black hole. He'd deliberately kept it that way, needing to emotionally distance himself from her after what had happened between them.

He'd told himself he'd find out where she was once he'd had time to get settled in London but he'd had a lot on his plate up till now. His business back in the States still needed a close eye kept on it until the chap he'd chosen to take over the CEO role in his absence was up to speed and he was keenly aware of his new familial duties here.

'My mother's staying with me at the moment so she'll be able to let me in,' Emma replied with a smile that didn't quite reach her eyes.

He nodded slowly, his brain whirring now. It occurred to him with a jolt of unease that he couldn't let her just skip off home. If she disappeared on him he'd end up looking a fool if the press came to call and he said something about their relationship that she contradicted later when they caught up with her. Which they would eventually.

And after not having seen her for nearly six years he had a thousand and one questions he wanted to ask her, which would continue to haunt him if she vanished on him again.

No, he couldn't let her leave.

'Look, why don't we go back to my house to talk? It's only a couple of streets away,' he said, wishing he hadn't dismissed his driver for the night. He hadn't intended to go out this evening but had been chivvied along at the last minute by an old friend from his university days who was a business acquaintance of Fitzherbert's.

'We need to figure out what we're going to do about this,' he said, registering her slight hesitation. 'You know what the gutter press are like in this country. We need to be able to give them a plausible answer if they come calling. If they think there's any kind of mystery about it they'll hound us for ever. I don't know about you, but I'm not prepared to have the red tops digging into my past.'

That seemed to get through to her and he saw a chink of acceptance in her expression. And trepidation.

He moved closer to her, then regretted it when he caught the sweet, intoxicating scent of her in the air. 'All I'm asking is that you come back to my house for an hour so we can talk. It's been a long time. I want to know how you are, Em.'

She looked at him steadily, her expression closed now, giving nothing away. He recognised it as a look she'd perfected after the news of her father's sudden death. He'd been a victim of it before, right after the tragedy had struck, and then repeatedly in the time that had followed—the longest and most painful days of his life.

'Okay,' she said finally, letting out a rush of breath.

Nodding stiffly, he pointed in the direction

they needed to go. 'It's this way,' he said, steeling himself to endure the tense walk home with his wife at his side for the first time in six years.

CHAPTER THREE

IT WAS A blessing that Jack's house was only two streets away because Emma didn't think she'd be able to cope with wearing his heavy wool coat so close to her skin for much longer, having to breathe in the poignantly familiar scent of him and feel the residual warmth of his body against her own.

It had been a huge struggle to maintain her act of upbeat nonchalance in front of him outside Jolyon's house and she knew she'd lost her fight the moment she'd seen the look in his eyes when he'd realised how cold she was. It was the same look he used to give her when they were younger—a kind of intense concern for her well-being, which reached right into the heart of her and twisted her insides into knots.

Gesturing for her to follow him, Jack led her

up the stone steps of the elegant town house and in through a tall black front door that was so shiny she could see her reflection in it.

The house was incredible, of course, but with a dated, rather rundown interior, overfilled with old-fashioned antique furniture in looming, dark mahogany and with a dull, oppressively dark colour scheme covering the walls and floors.

Jack's family had a huge amount of wealth behind them and owned a number of houses around the country, including the Cambridge town house overlooking Jesus Green and the River Cam that Jack and his sister, Clare, had grown up in. She'd never been to this property before though. They'd not been together long enough for her to see inside the entire portfolio of his life.

'What a—er—lovely place,' she said, cringing at the insincerity in her voice.

'Thank you,' he replied coolly, ignoring her accidental rudeness and walking straight through to the sitting room.

She followed him in, noticing that the décor was just as unpleasantly depressing in here.

'Was this place your grandfather's?'

'Yes,' he said. There was tension in his face, and a flash of sorrow. 'He left me this house and Clare the one in Edinburgh.'

Emma recalled how Jack had loved spending time with his grandfather, a shrewd businessman and a greatly respected peer of the realm. He'd always had an easy smile and kind word for her—unlike Jack's parents—and she'd got on well with him the few times she'd met him. Jack had notably inherited the man's good looks, as well as his business acumen.

'I was sorry to read about him passing, Jack,' she said, wanting to try and soothe the glimmer of pain she saw there, but knowing there wasn't any way to do that without overstepping the mark. He'd been very careful up until this point not to touch her and, judging by his tense body language, would probably reject any attempt she made to reach out to him.

She needed to keep her head here. This wasn't

going to be an easy ride for either of them, so rising above the emotion of it was probably the best thing they could do. In fact they really ought to treat this whole mess like a business transaction, nothing more, if they were going to get through it with their hearts intact.

The mere thought of what they had ahead of them made her spirits plummet and she dropped into the nearest heavily brocaded sofa, sinking back against the comforting softness of the cushions and pulling her legs up under her.

'Have you seen Clare recently?' she asked, for want of a topic to move them on from the tense atmosphere that now stretched between them.

'Not since Grandfather's funeral,' he replied, his brow drawn into a frown. 'She's doing well though—settled in Edinburgh and happy.' He looked at her directly now, locking his gaze with hers. 'She misses you, you know.'

Sadness sank through her, right down to her toes. 'I miss her too. It's been a long time since we talked. I've been busy—'

She stopped herself from saying any more,

embarrassed by how pathetic that weak justification sounded.

In truth, she'd deliberately let her friendship with Clare slip away from her.

A couple of months after Emma's father had passed away, Clare had gone off to university in Edinburgh and Emma had stayed at home, giving up her own place in an Art course there, which had made it easier to disassociate herself from her friend. Not that Clare hadn't put up a fight about being routinely ignored and pushed away, sounding more and more hurt and bewildered every time Emma made a lame excuse about why she couldn't go up to Scotland and visit her.

There had been a good reason for letting their friendship lapse as she had though. Clare hadn't known about her and Jack's whirlwind relationship. Emma hadn't known quite how to tell her friend about it at the time—in her youthful innocence she hadn't even known how to feel about it all herself—and she'd been sure Clare wouldn't have responded well to hearing how she'd snuck around with her brother behind her back, then how much she'd hurt Jack by walking away from their marriage.

Emma couldn't have borne being around her friend, whose smile struck such an unnerving resemblance to Jack's own it had caused Emma physical pain to see it, and not being able to talk about him to her. It would have been lying by omission. So instead she'd cut her friend out of her life.

The thought of it now made her hot with shame.

'How's your mother?' Jack asked stiffly, breaking into her thoughts.

She realised she was worrying at her nail, a habit she'd picked up after her father had died, and forced herself to lay her hands back in her lap.

'She's fine, thanks,' she said, deciding not to go into how fragile her mother had become after losing her wealth, good standing and her husband in one fell swoop. She liked to pretend none of it had happened now and had banned

Emma from talking about it. 'She's living in France with her new husband, except for this week—she's staying with me while Philippe's away and the house is being damp proofed and redecorated.'

Jack let out a sudden huff of agitation, apparently frustrated with their diversion into small talk. 'Do you want a drink?' Jack asked brusquely.

Clearly *he* did.

'Er, yes. Thanks. I'll have a whisky if you have it, neat.' A strong shot of alcohol would be most welcome right now. It was supposed to be good for shock, wasn't it?

Jack got up and moved restlessly around the room, gathering glasses and splashing large measures of whisky into them.

The low-level tension in the pit of her stomach intensified. She'd thought she'd be able to cope with being around him here, but his cool distantness towards her was making her nerves twang.

'So how's the electronics business in the good

old US of A?' she asked, wiggling her eyebrows at him in an attempt to lighten the atmosphere.

'Profitable,' was all he said, striding over to her and handing her a heavy cut-glass tumbler with a good two fingers of whisky in it.

'Are you trying to get me drunk?' she asked, shooting him a wry smile.

He didn't smile back, just turned away and paced towards the window to stare out at the dark evening.

Her heart sank. Where had the impassioned, playful Jack she'd once known gone? He'd been replaced with this tightly controlled automaton of a man. There was no longer any sign of the wit and charm she'd loved him so much for.

Knocking back a good gulp of whisky, she turned in her seat to face him, determined not to let her discouragement get to her. 'So you decided to come back and take on your social responsibilities as an earl, then?' She rolled the glass between her hands, feeling the pattern of the cut glass press into her palms.

He turned his head to look at her, his gaze un-nervingly piercing in the gloomy room.

'Yes, well, after being responsible for run-ning my own company for the last five years it's made me realise how important it is to uphold a legacy,' he said, folding his arms and leaning back against the window sill. 'How much blood, sweat and tears goes into building a heritage. My ancestors put a lot of hard work into main-taining the estate they'd inherited and it'd be ar-rogant and short-sighted of me to turn my back on everything they strove so hard to preserve.'

She was surprised to hear him saying this. She'd expected him to be reluctant to return to take on his aristocratic responsibilities after working so hard to achieve such a powerful po-sition in his industry.

But then for Jack it had always been about doing things on his own terms. From the sounds of it *he'd* made the decision to come back here; no one had forced him to do it.

She gave an involuntary shiver as a draught of cool air from somewhere blew across her skin.

Frowning, Jack left his vantage point at the window and paced over to the other side of the room, bending down and grabbing a pack of matches by the fireplace to light the tinder in the grate.

'So you're going to be living in England now?' she asked, her voice trembling as she realised what that would mean. There was a very good chance they'd see each other again, especially as Jack would be fraternising with the type of people they'd just left at the party. The worst of it was that she'd probably find herself serving him drinks and nibbles as a waitress at the society events he was bound to be invited to now.

'Yes, I'll be based in England from now on.' He sat back on his heels and watched the tinder catch alight, before reaching for a couple of logs from a basket next to him and laying them carefully over the growing flames.

Turning back to face her, he fixed her with a serious stare. 'So I guess we should talk about what we're going to do about still being married.'

Divorce.

That was what he meant by that.

She knew it was high time they got around to officially ending their marriage, but the thought of it still chafed. Dealing with getting divorced from Jack was never going to be easy, that was why she'd not made any effort to get in contact with him over the years, but the mere thought of it now made her stomach turn.

They'd been so happy once, so in love and full of excitement for the future.

She wanted to cry for what they'd lost.

'Yes. I suppose we should start talking to lawyers about drawing up the paperwork,' she said, desperately trying to keep her voice even so he wouldn't see how much the subject upset her. 'If that's what you want?'

He didn't say anything, just looked at her with hooded eyes.

'Are you—' she could barely form the words '—getting married again?'

To her relief he shook his head. 'No, but it's

time to get my affairs straight now I'm back in England.'

'Before the press interest in you becomes even more intense, you mean?'

She saw him swallow. 'Speaking of which, we need to work out what we're prepared to say to reporters about our relationship if they come calling.' He stood up and came to sit on the sofa opposite her. He was suddenly all business now, his back straight and his expression blank.

She took a shaky breath. 'Should we tell them we were married but we got divorced and we're just friends now?' The uncertainty in her voice gave away the fact that she knew deep down that that would never work.

He shook his head. 'They'll go and look for the decree absolute and see that we're lying. It'll only make things worse.'

Sighing, she pushed her hair away from her face. 'So what do we say? That our marriage broke down six years ago after you moved to the States, but we're only just getting round to finalising a divorce?'

'They'll want to know why you didn't go to America with me,' he pointed out.

'We could just say that I needed to stay here for family reasons,' she suggested, feeling a rush of uncomfortable heat swamp her as it occurred to her that they might go after her mother too.

'Well, at least that would be pretty close to the truth and it's better to keep things simple,' Jack said, seeming not to notice her sudden panic.

'It doesn't sound great though, does it?' she said, aware of her heart thumping hard against her chest. 'In fact it's probably going to pique their interest even more. They'll want to know what was so important here to make me stay and that'll mean dragging up my father's debts all over again.'

And if they did that Jack would find out she'd been keeping the true extent of them a secret from him for all these years.

After he'd left for the States she'd become increasingly overwhelmed by what she'd had to deal with and had eventually become so buried by it all she'd ended up shutting out everything except for dealing with her new responsibilities in order to just get through the day. Which meant, to her shame, that she'd shut Jack out too.

She'd been so young when it had happened though, only eighteen, and incredibly naïve about the way the world worked and how people's cruelty and selfishness kicked in when it came to protecting their wealth.

Not that there was any point in trying to explain all that to him now. Jack liked to feel he was in control of everything all the time and he'd probably only get angry with her for having kept him in the dark.

And anyway, there was no point getting into it if they were going to get a divorce.

She sighed heavily and put her head in her hands, massaging her throbbing temples. 'I don't know if I could bear having the press camped out on my doorstep, documenting my every move. And I know my mother certainly can't.'

'That might not happen,' Jack said softly.

'They may not even get wind of this. It depends on who overheard us at that party. But if they do find out about us I'll deal with it. If the question is asked we'll just say we got married on a whim when we were young and it didn't work out, but that we've always been on friendly terms and have decided to get a divorce now I'm back in England.'

She nodded her acceptance, feeling a great surge of sadness at how such a happy event could now be causing such problems for them.

Fatigue, chased on by the heavyweight alcohol, suddenly overwhelmed her and she hid a large yawn behind her hand, thinking wistfully of her bed.

The problem was, she was a long way from home and would need to take two different buses to get there. The thought of facing her mother's inquisitive gaze when she walked in made her stomach sink. She'd know immediately that something was wrong; the woman was particularly sensitive to changes in moods now after suffering with depression for years after her first husband's death.

Jack must have seen the worry in her face because he frowned and got up and came to sit down next to her.

'You're exhausted,' he said, the unexpected concern in his voice making the hairs stand up on her arms.

She shrugged, trying to make light of it. She didn't want him to think he had to mollycoddle her; she was perfectly capable of looking after herself. 'That's what happens when you work for a man like Jolyon Fitzherbert. He expects perfection from his employees. I've been up since five a.m. preparing for that party.'

Jack continued to look at her, his gaze searching her face.

Her stomach jumped with nerves as she forced herself to maintain eye contact with him, not wanting him to know just how fragile she was right now. He could probably blow her into dust if he breathed on her hard enough.

'Where do you live?' he asked.

She shifted in her seat. 'Tottenham.'

Not her first choice of places to live, but it was cheap.

'How were you planning on getting home?'

'We mere mortals take the bus.'

He ignored her wry joke. 'You can't take a bus all the way to Tottenham now. Stay here tonight, then we can talk again in the morning when we've both had a good rest and a chance to get over the shock of seeing each other again.'

She hesitated, on the brink of refusing his suggestion, but also keenly aware that if she left now she'd only have to psych herself up to see him again anyway, and probably somewhere much less convivial than here. Despite the terrible décor the house had the comforting atmosphere of a family home.

She realised with a shock that she'd missed the feeling of belonging somewhere, having lost her own family home and all the happy memories that went along with it when they'd been forced to sell it to pay off some of the debts.

So many memories had been tarnished by finding out the truth about her father.

She shook the sadness off, not wanting to dwell on it right now.

'Okay, thank you. I'll stay tonight and leave first thing in the morning,' she said.

He nodded, standing up. 'Good. The first bedroom you come to at the top of the stairs is made up for guests. Feel free to make yourself at home there.'

Make yourself at home. That wasn't something that was ever going to happen here, Emma reflected with another swell of sadness.

It was such a shame too. This house had the potential to be amazing if only someone showed it some love.

Not that she should be thinking things like that right now.

Pushing the rogue thought away, she stood up and brushed self-consciously at her skirt, trying to smooth out the still-sticky wrinkles. She must look such a mess, especially compared to Jack in his pristine designer shirt and trousers.

'Thank you,' she said stiffly. 'Could I use your phone? I'll need to let my mother know I won't be home tonight or she'll worry.'

'The landline's in the hall,' Jack said.

She gave him a stilted nod—how had things become so formal between them? They were acting like strangers with each other now—and made her way out to the hallway to find the phone.

It was telling that he hadn't lent her his mobile. Perhaps he didn't want her scrolling through his contacts or messages, nosing into his life. Was he trying to hide something from her? Or someone?

She didn't want to consider that eventuality right now; it would only increase the painful tightness she was experiencing in her chest and she needed all her composure if she was going to sound normal on the phone and not worry her mother.

It took a few rings before the line at home was picked up. From the sounds of her mother's voice she'd woken her up, so Emma quickly reeled off a story about Jolyon wanting her to work late and told her she was going to stay with a friend because she'd finish too late to get the last bus home.

At one point during the conversation, she heard Jack come out of the living room and mount the stairs, presumably going up to his room, and a layer of tension peeled away, making it easier to breathe.

From the tone of her mother's voice she could tell she wasn't convinced by the lie, but seemed to think Emma was ensconced in some clandestine affair instead. Which ironically wasn't far from the truth.

What would her mother say once she knew the truth? She'd be hurt, of course, that Emma hadn't felt she could confide in her, but the last thing she'd wanted to do right after her father's shocking death was add more stress to the situation by admitting to getting married to Jack without her mother's knowledge. And then when things had calmed down a little there had been no point in saying anything about it because things had fallen apart with Jack by then and she hadn't been able to see any way to fix them.

So she'd kept mum. In every sense of the word.

After saying goodbye to her mother, she made her way wearily up the stairs, turning onto the landing to find Jack standing outside the door of the bedroom she was meant to be staying in.

She came to a stop and stared at him in confusion. Why was he waiting for her here?

Unless…

'Were you listening to my phone call?' she asked, unable to keep the reproachful tone out of her voice.

'I was waiting to show you which room was yours,' he said, but she could tell from a slight falter in his voice that he was lying.

'You were checking that I wasn't calling a boyfriend, weren't you?' she said, narrowing her eyes.

He raised an eyebrow, refusing to be intimidated by her pointed accusation. 'I am still your husband, Emma.'

She folded her arms. 'Well, don't worry, you don't need to set the dogs on anyone. I haven't had a boyfriend since you left.'

There was a heavy pause where he looked at her with a muscle flicking in his clenched jaw. 'Since you decided not to follow me, you mean,' he corrected.

She sighed, feeling the weight of his resentment pressing in on her. 'I really don't want to argue with you right now, Jack. Can we discuss my failings tomorrow? It's been a very long day.' She forced herself to smile at him and went to walk past him, but he put an arm out, barring her way.

'Have you really not had another partner since we split up?'

Taking a breath, she turned to face him, feeling a small shiver run up her spine at the dark intensity she saw in his gaze. 'Well, my mother needed me for a long time after my father died and I've been working all the hours of the day to fit in both full-time work and night classes since then. So no. There hasn't been a lot of space for romance in my life.' She was aware of the bitter bite to her voice now and couldn't stop herself from adding, 'From what I've read in the press, it hasn't been the same for you though.'

When she'd first seen the articles about the high-profile relationship he'd had with the daughter of a famous hotelier six months after he'd moved to the States she'd had to rush to the toilet to be sick. She suspected it had been a deliberate move on his part to let her know that he'd moved on and that she hadn't broken his heart.

Even though she knew she had.

She'd heard the pain in his voice the last time they'd spoken to each other. The desperation, the frustration. But she'd had to harden herself to it.

They were never meant to be. The universe had made that very clear to her when it had killed her father.

Jack's eyes flashed with anger. 'Our relationship was over by then, Emma. You'd made that perfectly clear when you decided to stay in England with your mother instead of joining me, your *husband*, in the States.'

She took a calming breath, knowing that now wasn't the time to have a conversation about this when they were both stressed and still in shock from seeing each other again. 'I never meant to hurt you, Jack. Please believe that.'

He leant in towards her, his expression hard. 'I waited for you, Emma, like a fool, thinking you'd finally put us first once you'd had time to grieve for your father, but you never did.'

His gaze burnt into hers, his eyes dark with frustration.

'I know you took it all very personally, Jack, and I can't blame you for that, but I promise you it wasn't because I didn't love you. It was just the wrong time for us.'

He didn't respond to that, just kept looking at her with that unsettling, intense gaze of his.

'Goodnight, Jack,' she forced herself to say, moderating her tone so he wouldn't hear the pain this was causing her in her voice, and without waiting for his response she walked past him and shut the door.

Staggering into the room, her legs suddenly weak and shaky, she flopped down onto the large four-poster bed, its heavy mahogany frame squeaking with the movement, and curled into a ball, taking deep, calming breaths through her nose to stop herself from crying.

She understood why he was still upset with her. In his eyes she'd betrayed him, and Jack was not a man to easily forgive people who had hurt him. And she really couldn't blame him for so publicly cutting off their association at the knees, instead of letting it limp on painfully when there had been nowhere left for it to go.

Uncurling herself, she turned onto her back and stared up at the dark burgundy canopy above her.

Seeing him again, after all these years apart, made her heart heavy with a sorrowful nostalgia for the past. She'd grieved for Jack the same way she'd mourned her father at the time, only it had been a different kind of pain—with a sharp edge that constantly sliced into her well-being, reminding her that it had been her decision to end things with him and that there could be no going back from it. The damage had been done.

It had left a residual raw ache deep inside her that she'd never been able to shake.

Too tired now to even get undressed, she crawled beneath the sheets and let her mind run over the events of the evening. Her heart beat forcefully in her chest as she finally accepted that Jack was back in her life, although for how long she had no idea. He was obviously keen to get their 'situation' resolved so he could cut her completely out of his life and become available to marry someone more fitting of his position when the need arose.

She lay there with her thoughts spinning, suddenly wide awake.

In the first year after they'd parted she'd regularly tossed and turned in her bed like this, feeling so painfully alone that she'd given in to the tears, physically aching for Jack to be there with her, to hold her and whisper that everything would be okay, that she was doing a good job of dealing with the fallout from her father's death and that he was proud of her.

That he was there for her.

But he hadn't been.

Because she hadn't let him be.

A while after they'd split she'd considered moving on from him, finding someone new to love, but what with her intense working schedule and the mental rigor of taking care of her emotionally delicate mother there hadn't been room for anyone else in her life.

So she'd been on her own since Jack left for the States, and perhaps that had been for the best. She hadn't wanted to rely on someone else for emotional support after her father had let her down so badly, because that would have left her exposed and vulnerable again, something she'd been careful to put up walls against over the last few years.

At least on her own she felt some semblance

of control. She was the one who would make things better.

She turned over in bed and snuggled down further into the covers, hoping that fatigue would pull her under soon.

She'd find a way to deal with having Jack back in her life again. It would all be okay.

Or so she thought.

Waking early the next morning, her head fuzzy from a night of broken sleep and disturbingly intense dreams, Emma heaved herself groggily out of bed, wrinkling her nose at the smell of old booze on her crumpled clothes, and went to the window to see what sort of weather they had in store for them today, hoping for a bit of late autumn sunshine to give her the boost of optimism she needed before facing Jack again.

But it seemed that bad weather was to be the least of her problems.

Peering down at the street below her window, Emma realised with a sickening lurch that the pavement in front of Jack's house was swarming with people, some of whom were gazing up at the window she was looking out of as if waiting to see something. When they spotted her, almost as one, they raised a bank of long-lens cameras to point right at her. Even from this distance she could see the press of their fingers on the shutter buttons and practically hear the ominous clicking of hundreds of pictures being taken of her standing at Jack's window looking as if she'd just climbed out of his bed.

Leaping away from the window, she hastily yanked the curtains together again.

Someone at the party must have blabbed about what they saw and heard last night.

The press had found out about them.

CHAPTER FOUR

JACK HAD WOKEN EARLY, feeling uneasy about what he'd said to Emma the night before. He was annoyed with himself for losing his temper as he had, but hearing her practically accusing him of cheating on her had caused something to snap inside him.

He'd waited for *months* after moving to the States for word from her to let him know she was finally going to join him there, months of loneliness and uncertainty, only to finally be told, in the most painful conversation of his life, that she wasn't coming after all.

She'd given up on their marriage before it had even started.

He'd understood in theory that he'd been asking too much of her, expecting her to walk away from her life in England at such a difficult time, but he'd also been left with a niggling feeing that she'd chosen her mother over him and that she hadn't loved him enough to put him first.

After taking a quick shower and pulling on some clothes he strode down to the kitchen to set the coffee maker up, waiting impatiently for the liquid to filter through.

He was determined to stay in control today. There was no point in rehashing the past. It was time to move on.

Lifting a mug out of the cupboard, he banged it down on the counter. What was he thinking? He *had* moved on. Years ago.

But seeing Emma again had apparently brought back those feelings of frustration and inadequacy that had haunted him after he'd finally accepted she wasn't interested in being married to him any longer.

Sighing, he rubbed a hand over his face. He needed to get a grip on himself if he was going to get through this unscathed. The last thing he needed right now was Emma's reappearance in his life messing with his carefully constructed plan for the future.

He'd just sat down at the kitchen table with a mug of very strong coffee when she came hurrying into the kitchen, her eyes wide with worry and her hair dishevelled.

'What's wrong?' he asked, standing up on instinct, his heart racing in response to the sense of panic she brought in with her.

'The press—they must have found out about you being married because they're swarming around outside like a pack of locusts trying to get pictures.' She frowned and shook her head vigorously, as if trying to shake out the words she needed. 'They just got one of me peering out of my bedroom window at them—make that *your* bedroom window. I don't know whether they'll be able to tell exactly who I am, but their lenses were about a foot long, so they'll probably be pretty sharp images.'

He watched her start to pace the floor, adrenaline humming through his veins as he took in her distress.

Damn it! This was his fault for announcing their marriage to the whole of Fitzherbert's party last night. He'd been a fool to think they might get away with hiding from it. There was always going to be someone in a crowd like that that could be trusted to go to the papers for a bit of a backhander or the promise of future positive exposure for themselves.

'Okay. Don't panic, it might not be as bad as we think,' he said, reaching for his laptop, which he'd left on the table. Opening it up, he typed a web address into the browser and brought up the biggest of the English gossip sites.

He stared at the headline two down from the top of the list, feeling his spirits plummet.

The Earl of Redminster's Secret Waitress Wife! the link shouted back at him from the page.

He scanned the article, but there was no mention of Emma's name. 'Well, it can't have been Fitzherbert who tipped them off because they don't seem to know who you are. I guess he's kept his mouth shut out of embarrassment about the way he acted last night. Despite his drunken bluster, he won't want to get on the wrong side of the Westwood family in the cold light of day.'

He shut the laptop with a decisive *click*. 'Still, it looks like neither of us are going anywhere today. We can't risk going out there and having more photos taken of us until we've spoken to our parents and briefed them about what to say if any reporters contact them.'

She flopped into the chair opposite and raised a teasing eyebrow. 'What exactly do you intend to tell them, Jack? Funny story, Mum and Dad. You know how you thought your son was the most eligible bachelor in England? Well, guess what…?'

He tried and failed to stop his lips from twitching, gratified to see she wasn't going to let this beat her. Even so, he needed to keep this conversation on a practical level because this was a serious business they were dealing with.

'We can't hide from this, Emma, it'll only make things worse.'

She frowned at his admonishing tone. 'You

think I don't know that? It took years for the papers to stop rehashing the story about my father's debts. Any time high society or bankruptcy was mentioned in a story, they always seemed to find a way to drag his name and his "misdemeanours" into it.'

She sighed and ran a hand through her rumpled hair, wincing as her fingers caught in the tangles.

He stared at her in shock. 'Really? I had no idea they'd gone after your family like that,' he said, guilt tugging at his conscience. 'I didn't keep up with news in the UK once I'd moved to the States.'

What he didn't add was that after leaving England he'd shut himself off from anything that would remind him of her and embraced his new life in America instead. It seemed that by doing that he'd missed quite a lot more than he'd realised.

'Look, why don't you take a shower and I'll go and find you some fresh clothes to put on,' he suggested in an attempt to relieve the self-reproach now sinking through him. 'I'm pretty sure Clare keeps a couple of outfits here for when she visits London—they'll fit you, right? You were always a similar shape and height.'

The grateful smile she gave him made his stomach twist. 'That would be great. Yes, I'm sure Clare's stuff would fit me fine. Don't tell her I've borrowed it though, will you? She always hated me stealing her stuff.' Her eyes glazed over as she seemed to recall something from the past. 'I really do miss her, you know. I was an idiot to let our friendship fizzle out.' She paused and took a breath. 'But she reminded me too much of you,' she blurted, her eyes glinting with tears.

The painful honesty of her statement broke through the tension in his chest and he leant forward, making sure he had her full attention before he spoke. 'You should tell her that yourself. I'm sure she'd love to hear from you, even after all this time.'

Emma's gaze flicked away and she nodded down at the table, clearly embarrassed that he'd seen her flash of weakness. 'Yeah, maybe I'll do that.'

Standing up quickly, she clapped her hands together as if using the momentum to move herself. 'Right. A shower.'

He felt a sudden urge to do something to cheer her up. There was no need for them to be at each other's throats after all—what was done was done. In fact, thinking about it practically, it would make the divorce proceedings easier to handle if they were on amicable terms.

'When you come back down I'll make you some breakfast. Bacon and eggs okay with you?'

'You cook now?' Her expression was so incredulous he couldn't help but smile.

'I've been known to dabble in the culinary arts.'

She grinned back and he felt something lift a little in his chest.

'Well, in that case, I'd love some artistic bacon and eggs.'

'Great,' he said, watching her walk away, exuding her usual elegance, despite her crumpled clothes.

Out of nowhere, an acute awareness that she was still the most beautiful woman he'd ever known—even with her hair a mess and a face clean of make-up—hit him right in the solar plexus, stealing his breath away.

He thumped the table in frustration. How did she do this to him? Shake him up and make him lose his cool? No one else could, not even the bullying business people he'd battled with on a daily basis for the last few years.

Ever since the day he'd met her she'd been able to addle his brain like this, by simply smiling in his direction. As a teenager he'd been angry with her for it at first and to his enduring shame he'd treated her appallingly, picking at her life choices, her manners, the boyfriends she chose. Particularly her boyfriends.

The way she used to glide through life had bothered him on a visceral level. She was poised and prepossessing, and, according to his sister, the girl most likely to be voted the winner of any popularity contest at the eminent private girls' school they'd both attended in Cambridge. She'd seemed to him at the time to accept her charmed position in life as if it was her God-given right. He, on the other hand, had always prided himself on being subversive, bucking the trends and eschewing the norm and the fact she epitomised what others considered to be the perfect woman frustrated him. He hadn't wanted to be attracted to her. But he had been. Intensely and without reprieve.

What would it be like to hold her in his arms again, he wondered now, to feel her soft, pliant body pressed up against his just one more time, to kiss those sultry lips and taste that distinctive sweetness he remembered so well?

He pushed the thoughts from his mind.

The last thing they both needed now was to slip back into their old ways.

It could only end in disaster.

Even after a bracingly cool shower, Emma still felt prickly and hot with nervous tension.

Being here, in such close proximity to Jack, was playing havoc with her composure.

She knew it was necessary and practical to stay here today, but she had no idea how she was going to get through the day without doing or saying something she might regret—just as she had a few minutes ago in the kitchen when she'd blurted out why she'd deliberately cut contact with his sister.

Not wanting to dwell on that misstep right now, she dried herself and put on the clothes Jack had found for her and left out on her bed while she was in the en-suite bathroom.

The thought of him being in her room while she was naked next door gave her a twinge of nerves. He could so easily have come in when she was in there. Walked into the shower and joined her. If he'd wanted.

But clearly he didn't. And that was for the best.

It would be ridiculous to even contemplate the idea of anything developing between them again.

They'd be fools to think they could breach the chasm that had grown between them over the years. They were different people now. Wiser, older—harder, perhaps. More set in their ways. Certainly not young and carefree and full of excitement for the future as they had been right before they got married.

Twisting the necklace that had her wedding ring looped through it—something she'd never taken off, not in all the years they'd been apart—she gave it a sharp tug, feeling it digging into the back of her neck, reminding herself that any connection they'd once had was lost now and that she'd do well to remember that.

They would get a divorce and that would be the end of it. Then they could move on with their lives.

Trying to ignore the tension in her chest that this thought triggered, she turned on her heel and went downstairs to eat the breakfast Jack had promised her.

Passing through the hallway, she noticed that the handset had been left off the phone and it occurred to her that the press must have started calling by now to try and find out who she was and to hound them for details about their clandestine marriage.

It seemed Jack's plan was to ignore them for as long as possible.

Just as she thought this, the doorbell rang and continued to ring as if someone was leaning on it, determined not to stop until someone answered the door.

Damn press. They'd been the same way right after her father's death, hounding her and her mother for weeks, trying to get titillating sound bites or pictures that they could use in their repellent articles.

Hurrying out of the hall, she went straight to the kitchen to find Jack standing at the large range cooker, frying delicious-smelling bacon in a cast-iron pan.

It was such an anachronistic scene it made her tummy flip.

This was not how she'd pictured Jack whenever she'd allowed herself to think about him over the years.

Not that she'd allowed herself to do that too often.

When they'd been young and in love she'd thought of nothing but him: how it felt to be held in his arms, to be loved and worshipped by him. Then how it would be to live with him. Laugh with him every day. Grow old with him.

He was just as handsome now as he'd been when they'd got married, more so if anything. He'd grown into his looks, his face more angular, showing off that amazing bone structure of his, and his body harder and leaner than it had been in his youth.

She guessed he must have done regular power-gyming along with his power-businessing in the States. Wasn't that what all executives did now? Strong body, strong mind and all that.

'Something smells wonderful,' she said, walking over to where he was busy cracking eggs into the pan.

'It's my natural scent. I call it Eau de Charisma,' he said with a quirked brow as she came level with where he was standing.

She was so surprised that he'd made a joke, she instinctively slapped him gently on the arm in jest and just like that she was transported back in time, into a memory of Jack making her laugh like this the morning before they'd skipped off to the register office. She'd been trying to fix his tie and their fake squabbling had almost escalated into a rough and lustful lovemaking session on the kitchen table.

The memory of it hit her hard, chasing the breath from her body so that she had to back away from him quickly and sit down at the table, her legs suddenly shaky and weak.

What was wrong with her?

Couldn't she even eat breakfast without going to pieces?

Jack didn't seem to notice though and, after tipping their food onto bone-china plates, each one probably worth more than her entire stock of crockery at home, he brought them over to the table, placing hers in front of her without a word and sitting down opposite.

'Thank you,' she managed to murmur, and he nodded back, immediately tucking into his food.

Her appetite had totally deserted her, but she couldn't leave the food he'd so generously made for her, so she struggled through it, taking a lot of sips of tea to wash it past the large lump that had formed in her throat.

Neither of them spoke until their plates were clean.

Jack leant back in his chair and studied her, only making the jitters in her stomach worse.

Clearing her throat hard, she looked down and concentrated on straightening her knife and fork on the table until she'd got the feeling under control.

'Let's go and sit in the living room where it's more comfortable,' he suggested, and she nodded and got up gratefully, feeling a twang of nerves playing deep inside her.

* * *

Jack took the armchair near the fireplace and watched Emma as she fussed around the sofa she'd chosen to sit on, fluffing cushions and straightening the covers.

He felt stressed just watching her.

'Emma, why don't you sit down? I don't think that cushion's going to get any fluffier.'

Giving the offending article one last pat, she plonked herself onto the sofa opposite him and let out a low groan.

'I'm so full! There's a good chance I won't be able to move off this sofa now I've sat down, which is a worry because the view from here is giving me a headache.' She flashed him a speculative smile.

'Who decorated this place anyway? Please tell me it wasn't you,' she said with a glint in her eye. 'I really can't be associated with a man that thinks that aubergine and mustard yellow are good colour choices for what's meant to be a relaxing environment.'

He snorted in amusement. 'It was chosen by

my grandfather's assistant—who he was not so secretly bedding—and I haven't had time to change it since I've been back in England.'

She tipped her head to one side and studied him. 'I bet your place in the States was all cool chrome and marble without a speck of colour to be seen.'

He shrugged, a little stung by her pointed attack on his taste. 'I like my surroundings to feel clean and calming.' Despite his attempt not to sound defensive he could see from her expression that he hadn't managed it.

'Sterile, you mean.' She wrinkled her nose.

'Okay, Miss I-Have-Better-Taste-Than-You, what would you do to improve this place?'

'All sorts of things.' She got up again and walked around the room, peering around at the décor. 'Get rid of the awful dark wood furniture for a start. Put some warm heritage colours in here and some furniture to reflect the era in which the house was built, but with a modern twist.'

'A *modern twist*?'

She folded her arms and raised a brow. 'Yes. What's wrong with that?'

He grinned, amused by her pseudo outrage. 'Nothing. Nothing at all. I'm just not sure what a *modern twist* is. Do you mean you want to fill it with chrome and plastic?'

'No!' She slanted him a wry glance. 'Well, maybe a little of both, but only as accents.'

'Right,' he said, 'accents. Uh-huh.'

He realised with a shock that his earlier joke in the kitchen had brokered an unspoken truce between them and he was actually enjoying teasing her like this. It had been such a long time since they'd had a conversation that didn't end in one or both of them getting overly emotional, and it was comfortingly familiar to have a sparky back and forth with her again. He'd forgotten how fun it was to banter with her.

How? How had he forgotten so much? The gulf between them had been more than just a physical ocean, he realised; it had been a metaphorical minefield too, filled with piranhas. And quicksand. At least a galaxy wide.

They were both quiet for a minute, each seemingly lost in their thoughts.

Emma walked over to the mantelpiece and straightened the ugly carriage clock in the centre. 'Sorry,' she said when he glanced at her with an eyebrow raised. 'This is what stress does to me. It makes me want to tidy and clean things.'

'I know. I remember Clare telling me that you'd blitzed your whole house from top to bottom, including the attic, during your exams when you were seventeen.'

That had been about the time he was most struggling with his feelings for her. He'd been half relieved, half frantic when she'd failed to come over to their house to see Clare for two weeks during that time. It had made him realise just how strong his feelings for her were, which had only made him step up his condescension of her when she'd finally turned up again, looking fresh faced and so exquisitely beautiful it had taken his breath away. He also remembered the look of abject hurt on her face when he'd snapped at her for something totally inconsequential. And then what had happened as a direct result of it.

He was suddenly aware that he'd been staring at her while she stood there with a puzzled smile playing around her lips. 'You look awfully serious all of a sudden. What are you thinking about?' she asked, her voice soft and a little husky as if she'd read his thoughts.

He cleared his throat, which suddenly felt a little strained. 'Actually I was thinking about what happened after you came back to our house after going AWOL for those two weeks after your exams.'

She visibly swallowed as she seemed to grasp what he was talking about.

'You mean when you laid into me about how I'd supposedly flirted with the guy that was painting your parents' house and I decided to finally confront you about why you hated me so much?'

'Yes,' he said, remembering how she'd stormed up to his room after him and hammered on the door until he'd been forced to let her in. How she'd shoved him hard in the chest in her anger, the force of it pushing him against the wall, and how something inside him had snapped and he'd grabbed her and kissed her hard, sliding his hands into her silky hair and plundering her mouth, wanting to show her what she did to him and how much he hated it.

That was what he'd *actually* hated: his inability to control his feelings for her.

But instead of pushing him away, she'd let out a deep breathy moan that he'd felt all the way down to his toes and kissed him back, just as fiercely.

It had been as if a dam had broken. They couldn't get enough of each other's touch. He'd thought in those seconds that he'd go crazy from the feel of her cool hands on him. He'd wanted her so much, he'd ached for her. Desperate to get closer, he'd tugged at the thin T-shirt she'd been wearing, yanking it over her head until they were skin to skin. It had electrified him. He'd never felt anything like it before. Or since.

Getting up from the armchair, he went over to the fireplace to prod at a piece of charred wood that had fallen out of the grate, feeling adrenaline buzz through his veins from the intense mix of emotions the memories had conjured up.

'Jack? Are you okay?' She looked worried now and he mentally shook himself, angry for letting himself think about the past, something he'd been fighting not to do. For so, so long now.

'I'm fine,' he said tersely.

She recoiled a little at his sharp tone, looking at him with an expression of such hurt and confusion he had a crazy urge to drag her into his arms and soothe her worries away.

Fighting past the inappropriate instinct, he went over to the window to peer through a crack in the drawn curtains at the world outside to try and distract himself. The press were still milling around the front of the house, chatting and smoking and laughing as if they didn't have a care in the world.

Vultures.

'You know it won't be long until they find

out who I am,' Emma said behind him. She'd walked over to where he was standing and as he turned to face her the sweet, familiar scent of her overwhelmed him, making his senses reel.

He struggled past it, taking a couple of paces away from her and folding his arms.

Obviously a little stung by his withdrawal, she frowned and mirrored his stance, crossing her own arms in front of her.

'You're right. We should go to see our parents right away. I don't want to do it all over the phone—it's too delicate a situation. I'll call the car and we'll go to Cambridgeshire to see my parents this afternoon, then we can both go and see your mother together when we get back to London. We owe them that consideration at least.'

As if the mere mention of them had conjured them up, Jack's mobile rang and he glanced at the screen to see his parents' home phone number flash up.

A heavy feeling sank through his gut. This

didn't bode well. His parents rarely contacted him unless they needed something from him.

He pressed to receive the call. 'Father.'

'Jack? What the hell's going on? Apparently the press have got it into their heads that you're married to some down-and-out waitress! I've had a number of them already call the house this morning asking us to comment on it. Please tell me this ludicrous bit of gossip is unfounded!'

Judging by the strain in his voice, Jack could tell his father was not a happy man. This was the epitome of a disaster as far as Charles West-wood was concerned.

Jack took a steadying breath before answering. 'I am married. To Emma Carmichael. You remember her, she's Clare's best friend from school.'

There was a shocked silence on the other end of the line.

'Is this a joke?'

'No joke, Father. We got married six years ago, just before I moved to the States. We didn't tell anyone at the time because we thought both you and Emma's parents might try to stop us, thinking we were too young to know what we wanted.'

He actually heard his father swallow.

'Well, if she's Duncan Carmichael's offspring that makes total sense. That family was always good at wheedling what they needed out of people.'

Jack felt rage begin to build from the pit of his stomach. 'Emma can't be held responsible for her father's actions.'

His father let out a grunt of disdainful laughter. 'I'm surprised at you, Jack. I thought you were more savvy than to be taken in by a gold-digger.'

'I'll thank you not to speak like that about my wife,' Jack ground out.

'I'll speak any way I choose when it comes to the reputation of my family name,' his father said, his voice full of angry bluster. 'You need to come to the house *today* and explain yourself.'

'We were already planning on doing that,'

Jack said coldly, barely hanging onto the last thread of his cool. 'We'll be with you just after lunchtime.'

'Good. I hope for everyone's sake you're not letting this woman manipulate you. She could take a large part of your fortune if she decides to divorce you and we can't have our family's name brought into disrepute by having it dragged through the courts!' Before Jack could answer there was a click on the line as his father cut the call.

Jack stuffed his phone back in his pocket and turned to face Emma, who was staring at him with dismay on her face.

'They're expecting us,' he said unnecessarily. Clearly she'd heard the whole conversation judging by her expression.

'He thinks I married you for your money and that I'm going to take you for every penny you've got in the divorce,' she whispered, her voice raw with dismay.

Instinctively, he put a steadying hand on her

arm, feeling the heat of her skin warm his palm. 'It'll be fine. I'll deal with him and my mother. They're just in shock at the moment and don't know how to handle what little they've been told.'

She blinked and gave her head a little shake as if trying to pull herself together.

'Okay,' she said on a breathy exhalation, lifting her hands to smooth her already perfect hair down against her head. 'Well, I guess we'd better get ready to leave pretty soon if we're going to make it over there for after lunch. I'll call my friend Sophie now and ask her to bring my bag and coat here, then.'

Once again he found himself impressed with her cool handling of the situation. He hadn't expected her to be so composed about it all.

'Okay, you do that. I'll see you back down here in an hour and we'll hit the road.'

She gave him one last assertive nod and turned away.

He watched her go. Despite her fortitude he

was unable to shake the feeling that exposing Emma to his parents was tantamount to taking a lamb to the slaughter.

CHAPTER FIVE

THE THOUGHT OF seeing Jack's parents again fired adrenaline through Emma's veins as she walked out of the room to get herself ready to face them.

It had been years since she'd had any contact with the marquess and marchioness. They'd been quick to cut ties with her family the moment the news of her father's debts had broken, not even sending a card of condolence at his passing, and a little part of her hated them for that.

They'd known her quite well when she was a child, after all. She'd spent a lot of time at their house visiting Clare, but as soon as there was a hint of scandal attached to her she'd become persona non grata in their eyes.

And she was absolutely certain their opinion of her wasn't going to change any time soon.

Not that she particularly cared what they thought about her any more.

Unfortunately though, their interference still had the potential to make things very difficult for her if they decided she was a threat to them and their family's assets.

She was going to have to watch her back around them.

Shaking off the twinge of worry, she took a deep breath and went over to the phone in the hallway. She wouldn't worry about that now. There were more important things to give head-space to before they left for Cambridge.

The first thing she needed to do was call her boss, Clio, and let her know what had happened last night at Jolyon's house.

Clio picked up after a couple of rings and before she had a chance to say much, Emma launched into an abbreviated story of last night's debacle, quickly filling her boss in on the state of her and Jack's relationship and the complicated situation she found herself in now.

There was a pause on the line as Clio took a moment to digest all that Emma had told her before she spoke.

'It sounds like you had quite a night, Emma. Are you okay?'

Her boss's concern for her well-being above all else reminded Emma of why she loved working for her so much.

Even though she hadn't expected Clio to be angry with her it was still a relief to actually hear that she wasn't.

'I'm okay. Sort of. I'm not quite sure how this is all going to play out, but there's a good chance I won't be available to work for at least a week or two.'

'Don't worry about that,' Clio reassured her in soothing tones. 'I'll be able to find another job for you as soon as you're ready, Emma. You're one of my best girls; all the other clients you've worked for have sung your praises to me.'

Emma let out an involuntary sigh of relief. 'That's good to hear, Clio. Thank you.'

There was a pause on the line before her boss spoke again. 'You know, Emma, if you ever need to talk you give me a ring, okay? I'm always here if you need a listening ear.' She paused again. 'I had a similar experience myself a few years ago so I understand what you're going through.'

'Really?'

Emma was shocked to hear this. Her boss seemed so together, so focussed on her business. It was comforting to hear that someone she respected and looked up to so much wasn't infallible either.

'Are you secretly married too?' she asked tentatively.

Clio made a wryly amused sound in the back of her throat. 'Unfortunately it's not as straight forward as that.'

'When are relationships ever straight forward?' Emma said with a sigh.

'A good point,' Clio agreed.

There was a short pause. 'Listen, Emma,' Clio said carefully, 'for what it's worth, my advice is to keep in mind that just because the marriage wasn't right for you then, it doesn't mean it isn't right for you now. Both of you have had a lot of time to grow and learn things about yourself since then. That's worth considering.'

Emma's first reaction was one of scepticism that Jack would be at all interested in a reconciliation based on his angry outburst last night, but maybe Clio had a point. Sure, they'd grown apart over the years, each finding their own way forwards, but neither of them had gone so far as to ask the other for a divorce. And surely he never would have lost his cool with Jolyon if he didn't still care about her, at least in some small way?

Her heartbeat picked up as she cautiously entertained the idea of it. Even though he'd been standoffish around her since then, she couldn't help but wonder whether the more time they spent together, the more chance there was she'd spot a chink in his armour.

That there might still be hope for them.

But she'd be a fool to get too excited about the idea of it. There was probably too much water under the bridge now for them to turn things around.

Wasn't there?

'Anyway,' Clio said, breaking into her racing thoughts, 'like I said, don't worry about anything. Just let me know when you're in a position to take on another job and I'll make sure to find you something. In the meantime you take care of yourself, okay?'

'I will, Clio. And thanks. I really appreciate the support.'

She became aware of an achy tension building at the back of her throat and she concluded the call quickly so that her boss wouldn't hear the emotion in her voice.

She felt so confused all of a sudden.

After putting down the phone to Clio she took a moment to compose herself before calling Sophie, whose number she'd memorised because they'd worked so frequently together for the agency.

After giving her the same quick summary that she'd given Clio, she asked her friend to drop her missing bag and coat over to Jack's house, as she couldn't risk picking them up in person in case the press took more photos of her leaving.

Sophie's mixture of earnest concern and soothing support nearly set Emma's tears off again, but she managed to hold it together until they'd arranged how to get the missing items back to her.

Twenty minutes after she'd put the phone down to her friend there was a discreet knock at the back door where they'd agreed to rendezvous. Emma opened it to find Sophie waiting there with a look of worried anticipation on her face.

'One handbag, one coat,' Sophie said, holding the items up for her to grab as she dashed inside before any press noticed that she'd vaulted over the back wall and snuck through Jack's garden to gain entry.

'You're a lifesaver,' Emma said, giving her a tight hug.

'Are you okay?' Sophie asked, her voice muffled by Emma's hair.

It took Emma a moment before she was able to let go of her friend—the comfort of the hug seemed to be releasing some of the straining tension in her—and they drew away from each other.

Emma nodded, tried to smile, failed, then shook her head. 'Not really.'

'You poor thing. What a mess,' Sophie cooed.

'I know, and it's all of my own making. I should have contacted Jack before now...' she sighed and tugged a hand through her hair '...but I never seemed to find the strength to do it.'

'It must be a horrible thing to have to deal with. I don't blame you one little bit for letting it slide.'

'Well, there's no sliding out of it now. We're leaving to see his parents at their massive stately pile in Cambridgeshire in about ten minutes. I'll certainly be facing the firing squad there.

They're very uptight about how their family is portrayed in the media and I'm not exactly the daughter-in-law they were hoping for.'

'Emma, how can they not love you? You're an amazing woman, kind, compassionate, smart. They'd be lucky to have you as part of their family.'

Emma managed to dredge up a droll smile. 'Try telling Jack that.'

Sophie gave her a discerning look. 'You still have feelings for him, don't you?'

Emma sighed and rubbed a hand across her aching forehead. 'To be honest I don't know how I feel about him right now. He can be the most frustrating man in the world, but he does something to me on a visceral level, you know?'

'I do,' Sophie said, watching her with a worried frown. 'You can't help who you fall in love with.'

'No.'

They were both silent for a moment, each of them lost in their own personal reverie.

'Hey, do you have something knockout to

wear to meet his parents?' Sophie asked, breaking Emma out of her thoughts about how she was going to deal with spending more up-close-and-personal time with Jack when she was feeling so mixed up about him.

She glanced up at her friend. 'Jack's sister left some of her clothes here, which I can wear. They're a bit casual for a meeting with a marquess and marchioness, but they'll have to do. I haven't got time to go home now. Not that I've got anything suitable there either.'

'Okay, well in that case I'm glad I brought these with me.' Sophie slipped the strap of a suit carrier off her shoulder and held it out towards her.

'They're dresses I've just finished sewing for a charity catwalk show. You're so lovely and slim I think they'll fit you perfectly.'

The kindness of the act brought tears straight to Emma's eyes and she blinked hard, knowing that if she let as much as one of them fall she was a goner.

'That's so sweet of you, thanks,' she said, pulling Sophie in for another hug and holding onto her tightly until she'd got herself under control.

After disentangling herself, Sophie smoothed down her hair and gave her a warm smile. 'You're welcome. Knock their socks off, Emma! And call me as soon as you can to let me know that you're okay, all right. The girls and I were really worried about you when you disappeared like you did last night and they'll want to know you're in good hands.'

'I will. And thanks again, you're a good friend.'

'My pleasure, sweetheart.'

Blowing her one final kiss, Sophie nipped out of the door and hared back off across the garden before the paps got a chance to get a good look at her.

Shutting the door firmly behind her friend, Emma smiled and took a deep fortifying breath, thanking her lucky stars for such good friends.

It was so good to know that she wasn't completely on her own with this.

* * *

Jack was pacing the hall when Emma walked down the stairs to meet him looking a little pale, though still her poised, beautiful self. She was wearing a stunning dress, the structured soft grey material framing her curves in a way that made it impossible for him to drag his eyes away from her. There was something sharply stylish about the cut of it, even though the design was simple, giving the impression of confidence and effortless style. He had to hand it to her, she was a class act, even in the face of such a challenging situation.

In fact after what he'd witnessed in the last twenty-four hours it seemed he'd done her a disservice by assuming he'd have to handle the fallout from this all by himself. Instead of shying away from it, she'd stepped right up when it had become clear he needed her in this with him, and without one murmur of protest.

'My friend Sophie loaned it to me,' she said, following his gaze and fluttering her hands across the front of the dress. The strap of the handbag she was wearing over her shoulder slipped down her arm at the movement and dropped to the floor before she could catch it. As she bent down to pick it up something slipped out of the neck of her dress and flashed in the light as it twisted and swung around. He stared at the slim sliver chain. And the ring that was looped through it.

With a lurch of astonishment he realised he recognised it.

Her wedding ring.

She still wore it. Close to her heart.

Following his gaze, Emma looked down to see what he was staring at and when she realised what it was, she tried to stuff the necklace hastily back inside her dress again.

'You still have it,' he said, the words sounding broken and raw as he forced them past his throat.

'Of course.' She was frowning now and wouldn't meet his eye.

'Why—?' He walked to where she was standing with her hand gripping her handbag so hard her knuckles were white.

'I'm not very good at letting go of the past,' she said, shrugging and tilting up her chin to look him straight in the eye, as if to dare him to challenge her about it. 'I don't have a lot left from my old life and I couldn't bear to get rid of this ring. It reminds me of a happier time in my life. A simpler time, which I don't want to forget about.'

She blinked hard and clenched her jaw together and it suddenly occurred to him that she was struggling with being around him as much as he was with her.

The atmosphere hung heavy and tense between them, with only the sound of their breathing breaking the silence.

His throat felt tight with tension and his pulse had picked up so he felt the heavy beat of it in his chest.

Why was it so important to him that she hadn't completely eschewed their past?

He didn't know, but it was.

Taking a step towards her, he slid his fingers under the thin silver chain around her neck, feeling the heat of her soft skin as he brushed the backs of his fingers over it, and drew the ring out of her dress again to look at it.

He remembered picking this out with her. They'd been so happy then, so full of excitement and love for each other.

He heard her ragged intake of breath as the chain slid against the back of her neck and looked up to see confusion in her eyes, and something else. Regret, perhaps, or sorrow for what they'd lost.

Something seemed to be tugging hard inside him, drawing him closer to her.

Her lips parted and he found he couldn't drag his gaze away from her mouth. That beautiful, sensual mouth that used to haunt his dreams all those years ago.

A lifetime ago.

'Jack?' she murmured and he frowned and shut his eyes, taking a step away from her, letting go of the chain so that the ring thumped back against her chest, breaking the strange sensuous connection between them. This was crazy; he shouldn't be giving in to his body's primal urges, not with her. Not now.

It was too late for them. They were different people now. There was no point trying to re-hash the past.

'We should go,' he said, giving her a reassuring smile, which faltered when he caught the look of pained confusion on her face. 'We don't want to be late.'

Jack had arranged for his driver to pull up right outside the house and he and Emma—who had hidden her face behind a pair of Clare's old sunglasses and the brim of a baseball cap—practically sprinted to the car and flung themselves inside, determinedly ignoring the questions that were hurled at them from all sides.

Once safely in the back seat, Jack shouted for his driver to hit the gas and they left the pack of journalists behind them, scrambling for their own transport. Luckily his driver was able to shake them all off by taking a convoluted route through some back streets and when Jack checked behind them ten minutes later, there still wasn't anyone obviously tailing them.

They sat quietly, not speaking for the first part of the journey, and Jack took the opportunity to check work emails and calls. After he'd satisfied himself that everything was running smoothly without him, he sat back and looked out of the window, finally allowing his mind to dwell on the situation with Emma again, his thoughts whirring relentlessly.

Something had been bothering him since the phone call with his father, and it suddenly struck him what it was.

They'd be fools to think that trying to get divorced quickly would make all their problems go away. The press would be far more interested in them if they suddenly announced they were splitting up after their marriage had only just become news. His father would be sure to drag Emma's troubled past into the spotlight again, especially if he thought it would add weight to the Westwood's side of the claim in the divorce settlement. The man was capable of doing whatever it took to protect the family's estate.

He hated the idea of Emma having to go through the torture of being hounded by photographers again, having them hiding in her bushes and jumping out at the most inopportune moments. It would be incredibly stressful, especially if she had to cope with it on her own. At least when she was with him he could protect her from the majority of it, using the vast resources he had to hand.

The more he thought about it, the more an idea began to take shape in his mind. What if they stayed married, at least for the time being, and made out to the world that they were happy together? The press would soon grow bored with that—there wouldn't be any conflict in the story to get excited about. His father would be forced to leave her alone too if she retained the Westwood name.

Surely they could deal with being around each

other for a while longer, just until the interest in them had died down.

'Emma?'

'Hmm?' She turned to look at him with an unfocussed gaze as if she too had been deep in thought.

'What if we stayed married?'

Her gaze sharpened up pretty quickly at that.

'What do you mean?'

'I mean what if we pretend our marriage is solid? To everyone. Including our parents. That would give them time to get used to it and for the press interest in us to die down, then we could get divorced quietly and without anyone noticing in a few months' time.'

'A few months?' she repeated, as if she couldn't believe what she'd just heard and was a little unnerved by it.

'We'd only have to project a happy marriage in public—in private we could completely ignore each other if you like.' He knew he sounded defensive, but her sceptical response had rattled him.

Surely they could get past any awkwardness about being around each other again if it meant they'd be left alone to deal with this mess in a private and dignified manner. On their terms.

She seemed to be mulling the idea over now that she'd got over the initial shock of his suggestion, and she turned to face him again with a small pinch in her brow.

'You mean we'd live together in the same house?'

He took a breath. 'Yes, I guess that would make sense. To make it seem plausible that we're a happy couple, madly in love.' He was aware of tension building in his throat as he talked. 'You could move into my house. Just for those months. You'd be able to hide out there more easily than your flat and use my driver to get where you wanted to go.'

Turning away, she stared out of the window, her shoulders slightly hunched and her hands clasped in her lap.

'Okay,' she said so quietly he wasn't sure if he'd heard her correctly.

'Did you say okay?'

'Yes.' She swivelled to face him. 'I said okay. It makes sense to do that.' She paused to swallow, the look in her eyes a little circumspect. 'Just to be clear, you are talking about just being housemates, nothing more?'

He clamped his jaw together and nodded. 'Yes, that's what I meant.'

They'd be fools not to keep things strictly platonic between them; it would only complicate things if they didn't.

Sex hadn't even been on his mind when he'd made the suggestion. He'd been more concerned with protecting her from the press and keeping his own family out of the limelight.

He was thinking about sex now though.

That dress she was wearing was doing something unnerving to his senses. It accentuated her body in all the right places, making his blood race and his skin prickle as an urge to run his hands down it and trace her soft curves with his fingertips tugged at him.

Giving a small cough to clear the sudden tension in his throat, he gripped the handle of the door more tightly.

'I'm sure we can outwardly project the image that we're madly in love if we try hard enough,' she said quietly.

He twisted to look at her again, but she was staring out of the window again, her face turned away from him.

Sighing, he sat back in his seat and watched the countryside whizzing past, wondering exactly what they were letting themselves in for here.

The Westwood ducal estate was one of the most impressive in the country. Emma had heard that whenever the family opened their doors to the public, which wasn't often, they were so inundated with eager visitors there was gridlock in the roads around the estate for miles.

She would have been excited to have been invited to visit here under less stressful conditions, but as it was her stomach rolled with nerves as Jack's driver drove the car up the oak-tree-lined road to the front of the formidable-looking gothic stately home, with its geometric towers interspersed with harsh spires of grey stone, and came to halt in front of the grand entrance.

Jack's suggestion that they live together for the next couple of months had both terrified and electrified her.

The tense standoff at the bottom of the stairs earlier when he'd discovered that she wore her wedding ring around her neck seemed to have changed something between them. In that moment when he'd lifted it from around her neck she'd thought for a second he was going to kiss her. Her whole body had responded on a primitive level, her blood rushing through her veins and heating her skin in anticipation of the feel of his mouth on hers again after all this time.

The scary thing was, she'd wanted him to. So much.

Because then she'd know once and for all whether there was any way they could rekindle what they'd once had.

But he'd pulled away from her and the moment had disintegrated around them, taking any hope she might have had with it.

Until he'd just made the suggestion that they stay married, at least for a little while longer.

She could see that he was coming at it from a practical point of view, but, even so, she didn't think he would have suggested it if he didn't still care about her, at least a little bit.

Jack got out of the car and walked round to her side, opening her door and holding out his hand to her.

'Shall we?' Jack asked, his voice tinged with tension. Hearing that he wasn't entirely comfortable with being here either gave her that little bit of determination she needed to swing her legs out of the car, put her hand into his and stand up with a grace and dignity that she summoned from the depths of her soul.

They were in this together now.

He squeezed her fingers gently, as if hearing her thoughts, sending goose bumps rushing up her arm from where his warm skin made contact with hers.

'Okay. Are you ready?' he asked.

'As I'll ever be,' she said, dredging up a tense smile for him.

'Good. Remember, we're the ones in control here, not them.'

She let out a nervous laugh. 'If you say so.'

He nodded, his mouth twisting into a grim smile, and tugged gently on her hand, asking her to walk with him.

They'd barely made it halfway up the wide stone steps when the door was flung open and Jack's mother appeared on the doorstep, her perfectly coiffed chignon wobbling a little in her haste to get to them.

'Jack! Darling!' She tripped nimbly down the steps to meet them, the pearls around her neck swinging merrily from side to side. 'I'm so glad you're here.' Taking his face in her hands, she drew him towards her for a kiss on each cheek, then turned to Emma, giving her an assessing glance. 'It's good to see you again, Emma, dear.'

The wary expression in the marchioness's eyes made Emma think she wasn't being entirely truthful about the 'good' part.

'Come on in, we're all in the drawing room.'

All? Emma mouthed at Jack with a worried frown as his mother walked regally back up the steps, leaving them to follow in her wake.

Jack just shrugged, looking as confused as she felt.

Emma had never been in this house before. It had belonged to Jack and Clare's grandfather when she'd known them and she'd never been invited here. It was a breathtakingly impressive seat, with wide corridors filled with ancient paintings and artwork, leaning heavily on gold and marble to propagate the ridiculous wealth of the family.

'We're just through here,' the marchioness called over her shoulder, her voice sounding a little more strained now they were about to walk into what was bound to be the close equivalent of the Spanish Inquisition.

The room they walked into, with their hands

still tightly entwined and their postures stiff, was positively cavernous, with a soaring ceiling painted with gaudy frescos of angels frolicking in the clouds. Emma held her breath, her eyes scanning the room quickly to take it all in before she was forced to concentrate solely on the people that sat stiffly on the sofas positioned around the grand gothic fireplace in the centre of the room.

Which was why it took her a good few seconds to realise that there was at least one other friendly face in the room.

'Clare!' she gasped, dropping Jack's hand in her shock at seeing the woman she'd considered to be her best friend for most of the formative years of her life.

Clare stood up and walked towards them, her face breaking into a huge smile, a smile that flipped Emma's stomach with the warm familiarity of it.

'What are you doing here?'

'I happened to be visiting the olds and thought I'd stick around to greet my new sister-in-law.

Or apparently not so new,' her friend said, her lips twisting into a wry, quizzical smile.

'It's so good to see you,' Emma said, burying her face in her friend's curly auburn hair and breathing in the comfortingly floral scent of her. 'I've missed you,' she whispered fiercely into Clare's ear, pulling back to look into her face so her friend could see just how sincerely she meant that.

'I've missed you too, Em,' Clare said, her eyes glinting with tears.

'Well, Jack,' Clare said, turning to give her brother the same perplexed smile, 'you've pulled some crazy stunts in your life, but I never thought getting secretly married to my best friend would be one of them.'

Jack smiled at her with a pinch in his brow as if trying to figure out how best to frame his answer.

'How—? I mean, when—?' Clare shook her head and took a breath. 'I mean *how* did I not know about this? I'm beginning to worry I've been abducted by aliens and had six years' worth of memories erased or something.'

A lead weight of guilt dropped into Emma's stomach.

Jack advanced towards his sister and pulled her into a tight hug before releasing her to look her in the eye.

'I'm sorry we didn't tell you, Clare. I feel terrible about keeping you in the dark all this time.'

Emma put her hand on Clare's other shoulder. 'I'm sorry too, sweetie. I should have told you when it happened, but I—' She looked down at the floor and shook her head. 'I guess I got a bit carried away with the romance of it all and I had no idea how to explain my feelings for Jack to you. To be honest, I was terrified you'd hate me for falling for your brother. The last thing I meant to do was hurt you.'

'Yes, yes, this is all very touching, but I'd like to hear how this all came about,' said a deep, penetrating voice from the corner of the room.

Emma turned to see Jack's father, Charles

Westwood, Marquess of Harmiston, advancing towards her.

'Emma,' he said, giving her a curt nod.

She wondered for a second whether he expected her to drop into a curtsey.

Well, he could expect all he wanted, there was no way she was going to pander to him.

'My Lord,' she said, keeping her chin up and her back straight. 'Thank you for welcoming me here today. I can imagine how upsetting it must have been for you to hear about Jack and I being married the way you did, and I apologise for that.'

Something flickered in the man's eyes, but his expression remained impassive.

'Are you going to tell us why it's been kept such a secret for all this time?' he asked, his tone strident now.

Before she could speak, Jack stepped up next to her to address his father.

'As I mentioned on the phone, we started a relationship when Emma was seventeen and I was twenty, but we decided to keep it quiet at the time because we wanted time to explore it without our families sticking their noses into our business.'

Jack let that hang in the air for a moment before continuing.

'Then when I got the offer from the States to go and work out there I decided I wanted Emma to go with me and the easiest way to make that happen was for us to get married.'

His father raised a censorious eyebrow and looked as though he was about to say something, but Jack ignored him and carried on speaking.

'Unfortunately Emma's father passed away right after the wedding ceremony so it became impossible for her to follow me out there and I'm sad to say our relationship drifted after that. In retrospect we realise we weren't emotionally mature enough at the time to make it work then.'

She felt his arm slide around her shoulders and forced herself to relax into his hold, as a woman who felt loved would, despite the awareness that Jack must be struggling not to add that he actually believed she'd abandoned him.

'We've stayed in contact over the years and since I've been back in England we've decided to reconcile our marriage,' Jack continued, still not looking at her. Even though he looked outwardly relaxed she would swear she could feel the underlying tension in his hold on her.

To her surprise, Clare moved quickly towards them and wrapped her arms around her and Jack, dragging them all into an awkward group hug.

'Well, I couldn't be happier for you both. Honestly. I always thought you'd make a great couple. You were always so sparky together. And now there's definitive proof that I'm *always right*,' Clare said, grinning at them both.

Emma forced herself to grin back, her scalp feeling hot and tight as her friend's misplaced enthusiasm caused a stream of discomfort to trickle through her.

She pushed the feeling away. Now wasn't the time to feel guilty about what they were doing.

'Well, now that's all straightened out I sup-pose we can relax a little,' the marchioness said in a rather brusque voice.

Clearly she didn't share Clare's joy at the news that she now had a waitress with a tarnished reputation for a daughter-in-law for the fore-seeable future.

Jack's father didn't say anything, just looked at them with a disconcerting smile playing about his lips, as if he suspected there was more to it than they were telling him.

Shrewd man.

And a dangerous one. Emma could see now why Jack had wanted them to show a united front. Judging by the look of cold distrust in the marquess's eyes, Emma imagined the man would happily feed her to the wolves, given half a chance.

Well, at least it was over with now and they could go back to London without the fear of Jack's parents interfering in their relationship.

A loud ring of the doorbell made them all start in surprise.

'Ah, that will be Perdita,' the marchioness said, rising from her chair.

A moment later a deathly pale woman with a shock of white-blonde hair and the palest eyes Emma had ever seen was shown into the room by a butler, followed by a man with a camera slung around his neck.

'Perdita is our good friend and a journalist from *Babbler* magazine,' Jack's mother announced to them all with a cool smile. 'She's going to do a lovely feature for us showing how invested we all are in your marriage and how excited we are about welcoming you into your place in our family, Emma.'

CHAPTER SIX

'WHAT THE HELL is this?' Emma heard Jack growl under his breath to his father as his mother tripped over to greet her friend with an exaggerated air kiss.

Emma knew exactly why he was so angry. The more fuss they made about being a happily married couple, the harder it would be to let the relationship dissolve without a lot more press attention.

'Surely you don't mind having people know how happy you are to be married to each other?' his father said loudly with a glint of devilry in his eyes.

He had them trapped. There was no way they could refuse to do this without it looking suspect. Clearly Jack knew that too because he gave her an extra hard squeeze as if asking her to play along.

She turned to smile at him. 'Of course we don't mind, do we, darling?' she said, hoping her expression relayed her understanding of the situation to him and her acceptance of it.

A whole conversation passed between them in that look and Jack finally nodded curtly and turned to the new additions to their group and said, 'What exactly did you have in mind?'

'We only have time for a couple of photos today if we're going to squeeze you into the next issue, but I'll come over to your house in a week or so and do a more in-depth interview for an *"At home with the Earl and Countess of Redminster"* feature,' Perdita said in a gush of fawning enthusiasm. 'For starters I'd like to get some lovely shots of the happy family together.'

Reluctantly, they allowed themselves to be herded into a tight group in front of the looming marble fireplace in the centre of the room and Emma found herself standing between the marquess and marchioness, pressed up tightly to Jack, with her back flat against his broad chest and his arms wrapped around her waist.

'Love's young dream!' Perdita gushed, giving them an insipid smile that made Emma squirm inside.

Heat rushed through her as she felt Jack shift behind her, his arms tightening infinitesimally to press a little harder into her pelvis, only increasing the heavy pounding of her heart. The fresh, exotic scent of his aftershave mixed with his own unique scent enveloped her, making her head swim.

He'd always smelled good. More than good. In fact in her younger days after being with him she used to hold the clothes she'd been wearing up to her nose and breathe in his lingering scent. She'd not been able to get enough of it.

She still had one of his old sweaters at home that he'd loaned to her one day when they'd gone on a cold walk together, just days before they were married, which she'd deliberately not given back so she could sniff it at home like some kind of Jack junkie.

She remembered with a twang of nostalgia how full of hope she'd been that day, how excited about their future together. The intensity of her love for him had taken her breath away, robbed her of all common sense, made her dopey with happiness.

The day she'd married him had been the best day of her life—and the worst.

She could still remember the feeling of absolute horror and helplessness when she'd arrived home after their clandestine marriage—her one and only rebellion in a life of respectful rule-following—ready to tell her parents that she was going to move to America to build a life with Jack there, only to find her mother prostrate on the sofa, her face a sickly white and her eyes wild with grief. She'd rushed to her, panicked by the look on her face, and her mother had told her in a broken voice filled with tears that her father was dead.

She'd spent the next few hours desperately trying to hold herself together for the sake of her mother, who had totally fallen apart by then, as if Emma's appearance had released her from the responsibilities of dealing with her husband's death.

In her state of shock she'd ignored the calls on her mobile from Jack, who had been waiting impatiently for her to meet him in the hotel room they'd booked, where they had been going to celebrate their wedding night together.

Eventually she'd called him, finding him in a state of frantic worry, and explained what had happened, feeling as though she was looking down at herself from above. Jack had wanted to come over and be with her, to help in some way, but she'd told him no, that it would only distress her mother more to have him in the house and that she didn't want to have to explain his presence there. She wasn't going to tell her they were married, it wasn't the right time.

That moment was the point at which their relationship had begun to unravel. She recognised it now, in a flash of clarity. She'd pushed him away, rejecting his love and support, and it had hurt him more deeply than she'd realised at the time.

So it was absolute torture, standing there enfolded in his arms once again, but this time having to fake their love for the camera so that strangers could gawp at their lives as if it was entertainment.

If only her father hadn't died, maybe they would have still been blissfully happy together today.

If only…

But there was no point in wishing she could change the past. It was futile and a waste of energy. Instead she needed to look to the future with positivity and have faith that she'd find happiness again there.

'Ooh, that's a lovely one,' Perdita purred from the other side of the room as her photographer snapped another shot and it appeared on the screen of a laptop Emma had seen him toying with earlier.

'Let's just have one of the happy couple on their own now, shall we?' Perdita said with a cajoling lilt to her voice. Emma thought she and Jack had been doing a convincing job of looking comfortable with each other, but there was a strange gleam in the journalist's eye that she didn't like the look of. Did she suspect all wasn't quite as it seemed? Probably. It was her job to see past people's façades and get to the heart of a story, after all.

Emma swallowed hard, but managed to keep her smile in place.

The rest of Jack's family moved away from the stiff tableau they'd formed for the photo and went to perch on the nearby sofas to watch the rest of the show.

'When will the next issue of the magazine come out, Perdie?' Jack's mother asked, her eyes glued to the way Jack's arms were still wrapped around Emma's middle as if she was looking for something to criticise.

'In a couple of days. We'll just be able to squeak them into the next issue along with some upbeat captions about them renewing their vows.'

Jack's arms tightened around her and her heart jumped in her chest in response.

'What makes you think we're going to renew our vows?' he snapped.

'I told Perdita that's what was going to happen, dear,' Jack's mother broke in. 'It's such a *prudent* course of action, what with being so suddenly reconciled after all this time. And it means all your friends and family will be able to celebrate your union with you this time.' Despite the cajoling note in her voice Emma clearly heard the undertone of steel in her mother-in-law's words.

Jack didn't say anything more, but she could practically feel the waves of frustration rolling off him.

'The full interview will be in the next issue because there just isn't room for it in this one and we'll want to do a nice big spread,' Perdita went on gaily, apparently enjoying the drama that was unfolding in front of her. Emma guessed she could see a whole career's worth of titillating stories in the offing.

'I had a fight on my hands finding some room for these pictures, to be honest,' Perdita went on. 'We had to bump a spread on Fenella Fenwicke's third wedding.'

Tripping over to where she and Jack stood shifting uncomfortably on their feet, she put a cool hand onto Emma's wrist.

Emma had to work hard not to whip her arm away from the clingy covetousness of the woman's grip.

'Now then. Shall we have one of the two of you looking adoringly into each other's eyes? That should play well with our readers.'

Emma's heart sank. She was going to have to look into Jack's eyes with the same insipid expression she'd been struggling to maintain for the past twenty minutes and still hold it together.

What if he saw past her nonchalant façade and noticed how she was desperately trying to hide how much she still cared for him? And what if he didn't actually care about her any more and she saw it there clearly in his face?

How would she cope when all these people were watching them?

Taking a breath, she steeled herself against her trepidation and turned around to look at him.

Jack looked back at her, his green-flecked hazel eyes filled with an unnerving intensity behind his long dark lashes.

Emma's heart thumped hard against her chest as she forced herself not to break eye contact with him.

He was so outrageously handsome it dragged the breath from her lungs.

But handsome didn't keep her warm at night, she reminded herself. It didn't make her feel secure and loved, wanted and treasured.

Safe.

Falling in love was a precarious business, full of hidden dangers and potential heartbreak, and she didn't know if she could bear the idea of being that vulnerable again. Not when she'd already experienced how quickly and catastrophically things could go wrong.

After a few more seconds of torture, Jack and Emma holding the same pseudo loving pose for the camera, Perdita finally clapped her hands together and gave a tinkling little laugh.

'That's it! Perfect. I think we have all we need for now.' She turned to Jack's mother. 'I'll let you know when the issue with the pictures is out, Miranda.'

'Thank you, Perdie. You're a good friend.'

And a shrewd businesswoman, Emma thought with a twinge of distaste. Those pictures would probably be worth a fortune if she leaked them to the papers, not to mention the career-enhancing glory of getting the scoop for her magazine.

'I'll call you about setting up that *at home* interview in a couple of days,' she shouted across to Jack and Emma as she bustled about, gathering up her bag and laptop.

After another minute of fussing and gushing pleasantries with the marquess and marchioness, Perdita finally left in a flurry of kisses and a blast of expensive perfume and the atmosphere in the room settled into an unnerving hum of prickly discontent.

Jack had had enough of his parents' intrusion into his affairs.

'Right, well, now this circus is over we'll be leaving,' he said to them.

'Wait, Jack, why don't you stay a little longer so we can get to know our new daughter-in-law a bit better?' his mother said in an appeasing tone, bustling over to where he and Emma stood.

He didn't like the glint of mischief in her eyes. No doubt she would spend the time grilling Emma in the hope of getting her to admit to something they could use against her later.

There was no way he was letting that happen.

'You got what you wanted. We put on a good show for the sake of your image as invested parents-in-law, so now you can leave us alone,' he snapped.

'Jack, we just want what's best for the family—' his father began.

'No, you don't,' Jack broke in angrily, 'you want what's best for you. Well, I'm doing what's best for *us* and that means getting the hell away from this toxic atmosphere. Come on, Emma.' He held out his hand to her.

She took it, wrapping her fingers tightly around his, and he was alarmed to feel how much she was trembling.

She'd projected such an outwardly cool exterior throughout the whole debacle he was surprised to discover she seemed to be suffering just as much as he was.

'I'm sorry to leave so suddenly, Clare,' he said, turning to his sister.

He was grateful that she'd stuck around to be here today. It had been good to have another ally for Emma in a strained situation like this.

And he was glad for the opportunity to see his sister again; he'd missed her open smile and level-headed, easy company while he'd been living away in the States.

Clare gave them both an understanding smile. 'You must both come up to Edinburgh soon,' she said, her expression telling him there was no way she was letting them get away without seeing her for that long again.

He just nodded at her, uncomfortably aware that he and Emma might not be together for very much longer so there was no point in trying to arrange anything with his sister for the future.

He'd work out how to handle all that later though.

Right now he wanted to get Emma out of there and as far away from his parents as possible.

They left without another word, Jack aware of his parents' disgruntled gazes on his back but not giving a fig how they felt about him laying down the law to them. No way was he going to let them try to run his life.

Back outside he opened the passenger door for Emma and watched her slide into the car, as graceful as ever—struck by how even in the most difficult situations she still managed to maintain her poise—then went round to the other side of the car and got in next to her.

They drove away in silence, Emma watching out of the window as the car made its way down the long driveway, glancing back to look at the house as if concerned that his parents might come out and hotfoot it after them.

She caught his eye and he gave her a tight smile, which she returned.

'Are you okay?' he asked her, half expecting her to shout at him now for putting her through that. 'I'm sorry about them landing a journalist on us like that. I know how you must hate them after what they did to your family when your father died.'

'It wasn't your fault, Jack. It's fine,' she said, but he was sure he saw a glimmer of reproach in her eyes.

For some reason her controlled restraint bothered him. He realised he actually wanted her to rage at him, so he could rage back at her. To get all the pain and anger out in the open, instead of all this polite pussyfooting around they were doing.

Instead, he took a deep breath and told himself to calm down. His parents' meddling was no fault of hers. Or his.

But as he stared out of the window the memory of having to stand in full view of his family and look lovingly into Emma's eyes came back to haunt him, crushing the air from his lungs. He could have sworn he'd seen something in her gaze, something that made his heart beat faster and his blood soar through his veins.

It had made him nervous.

He still felt twitchy and wound up from it now and a sudden urge to get out of the confines of the car and walk around for a minute to get rid of his restless energy overwhelmed him.

'We should stop and get a drink somewhere before we head back to London,' he muttered, and before Emma could protest he leant forwards and asked John to stop at the country pub that was coming up on their left.

Once they'd pulled into the car park he said, 'Let's take a quick break here,' getting out before she had chance to answer him.

The temperature was cool, but the sun was

out and Jack felt it warm the skin of his face as they walked towards the pub. It was a relief to be outside again. Despite the impressive dimensions of the rooms in his parents' house he'd felt claustrophobic there and had been hugely relieved to leave its austere atmosphere.

The exterior of the pub had already been decorated for Christmas and strings of fairy lights winked merrily at them as they walked up to the front of the building.

'Let's sit out in the beer garden,' he suggested as they came to a halt at the front door. He could already imagine how the dark cosy interior would press in on him. He needed air right now.

'Sure, okay,' Emma said, slanting him a quizzical glance.

'I just need to be outside for a while.'

She nodded. 'Okay, I understand. I'll go and get the drinks. What would you like?'

He frowned. 'No, I'll get them.'

Putting up a hand, she fixed him with a determined stare. 'Jack, I can stretch to buying us a couple of drinks. Let me get them.'

Knowing how stubborn she could be when she put her mind to it, he conceded defeat. 'Okay, thanks. I'll have an orange and soda,' he said, aware he needed to keep his wits about him, despite an almost overwhelming craving for a large shot of whisky to calm his frazzled nerves.

'Okay, you go and find us a good table in the sun. I'll see you out there,' she said, already heading into the pub.

He found a bench right by a small brook in the garden and sat down to wait for her to return, watching the fairy lights twinkling in the distance. Barely a minute later he spotted her striding over the grass to join him, a drink in each hand. It looked as though she'd gone for the soft option as well.

He was surprised. He'd expected her to come back with something much stronger after having to deal with the nonsense his parents had subjected her to.

A sudden and savage anger rose from somewhere deep inside him—at his parents, at her, at the world for the twisted carnage it had thrown at them both.

She put the drinks carefully down on the table like the good little server she'd become.

It burned him that she hadn't done anything worthwhile with her life when there had been so much potential for her to do great things with it.

Instead she'd given up her life with him in the States for what? To become a *waitress*. At this last thought his temper finally snapped.

'Why the hell are you wasting your time working in the service industry? I thought your plan was to go to university to study art and design,' he said roughly, no longer able to hold back from asking the question that had been burning a hole in his brain since he'd first seen her again.

Her initial shock at his abrasive tone quickly flipped to indignation.

'Because I've had to work to pay off my father's debts, Jack,' she blurted, sitting down heavily opposite him, clearly regretting her loss of control as soon as the words were out.

He stared at her in shock. *'What?'*

She swallowed visibly but didn't break eye contact. 'They were rather more substantial than I told you they were, but I was finally on track to pay off the last of them—until I lost my job yesterday.'

Guilt-fuelled horror hit him hard in the chest. 'Why didn't you tell me? You said the money from the sale of your family house had taken care of the debts your father left.'

Frustration burned through him. If she'd told him she needed money he would have offered to help. Not that she would have taken it from him at that point, he was sure. After her father's death she'd sunk into herself, pushing everyone she'd loved away from her. Including him.

'It wasn't just the banks he owed money to,' she said with a sigh. 'He'd taken loans from friends and relatives too, who all came out of the woodwork to call the debts in as soon as they'd heard he'd passed away.'

Jack frowned and shook his head in frustration. 'Emma, your father's debts weren't yours to reconcile all by yourself.'

She shrugged and took a sip of her drink before responding. 'I didn't want to be known for ever as the poor little rich girl whose daddy had to borrow money from his friends in order to keep her in the lifestyle to which she'd become accustomed, who then ran to her rich husband to sort out her problems.'

The pain in her eyes made his stomach burn. He went to put a reassuring hand on her arm but stopped himself. He couldn't touch her again. It might undo something in him that he was hanging onto by a mere thread.

'I didn't want you to have to deal with being hounded by the press too,' she added in a small voice. 'You had enough on your plate what with starting at your new job.'

He thought again about how he'd avoided seeking out any news from the UK after moving to the States. The cruel irony of it was, if he hadn't done that he'd have been more aware of how her father's name had been dragged through the press and what she'd been put through after he'd left. And ultimately that would have helped him understand why she'd shut him out of her life once he'd moved away.

'I'm sorry I didn't tell you the whole truth, Jack, but I was overwhelmed by it all at the time. I guess I was too young and naïve to deal with it properly. It felt easier just to shut you out of it,' she said suddenly, shocking him out of his torment.

He felt a sting of conscience as he remembered his angry rant at her the other night.

'I know I promised I'd put us first once things had settled down but sorting out the carnage that my father had left us to deal with took up my every waking second, my every ounce of energy. I felt adrift and panicky most of the time, lost and alone, and I couldn't see past it. There didn't ever seem to be an end in sight.'

She took another sip of her drink but her hand was shaking so much some of the liquid sloshed over the edge of the glass and onto the table.

'Every day after you'd gone I told myself that I'd call you tomorrow, that once things had settled down I'd get on a plane and go and find you, but they never did.'

She mopped absently at the spillage with a tissue that she'd pulled out of her bag.

'Months bled into each other until suddenly a whole year had passed and by that time it felt too late. I'm sorry I let things drag on the way I did, but I didn't want to have to face the reality that there couldn't be any *us* any more. That my life with you was over. You were everything I'd ever wanted but I had to let you go. I didn't feel I had any choice.'

She rubbed a hand across her forehead and blew out a calming sigh. 'The other problem was that my mother wasn't well after my father died. She became very depressed and couldn't get out of bed for a long time. I needed to be there for her twenty-four hours a day. To check she wasn't going to do anything—' She paused, clearly reliving the terror that she might come back home to find herself an orphan if she left her mother alone for too long.

Jack nodded and closed his eyes, trying to make it clear he understood what she was telling him without her needing to spell it out.

Dragging in a breath, she gave him a sad smile. 'So it was left to me to organise the funeral, arrange the quick sale of the home I'd lived in since I was a little girl and face the angry creditors on my own while my mother lay in bed staring at the wall.'

'I could have helped you, Emma, if you'd let me,' he broke in, feeling angry frustration flare in his chest.

'I didn't want you involved, Jack. I was hollowed out, a ghost of my former self, and I didn't want you to see me like that. You would have hated it. I wanted to be sparkling and bright for you but my father's death drained it all away.' She sighed. 'Anyway, it was my family's mess, not yours.'

He leaned in towards her. 'I was your family

too, Emma. Not by blood, but in every other way. But you pushed me away.'

She took a shaky-sounding breath. 'I know my decision to stay in England hurt you terribly at the time, but my mother needed me more than you did. She would have had no one left if I'd slunk off to America and there was no way I could just leave her. There was no one else to look after her. All her friends—and I use the word in the loosest of terms—abandoned her so they didn't find themselves tainted by our scandal.'

Her voice was wobbling now with the effort not to cry. 'I know that my father would have expected me to look after my mother. He would have expected us to stick together. I didn't want to dishonour his memory by running away from our family as if I was ashamed to be a part of it.'

She held up a hand, palm facing him. 'I accept that he made mistakes, borrowing all that money, but I believe he did it in order to make his family happy. So I've spent the last six years working hard to pay off his debts. To finally clear our name—'

Her voice caught on the last word and Jack shifted in his seat, distraught to hear how much she'd suffered in silence, but he didn't speak, letting her keep the floor, sensing how much she needed to let it all out now.

'I didn't want you to be dragged down by the mistakes my father made too. It wouldn't have been fair on you when you were so excited about taking that amazing job offer in America. I knew it was a once in a lifetime opportunity, and how determined you were to shun the unfair advantage of your family name and do something great with your life on your own merits. It would have been cruel of me to take that chance away from you, Jack.'

'There would have been other opportunities though, Emma. I was more concerned about the two of us making a new life for ourselves *together*,' he broke in, before he could stop himself.

She sighed and rubbed at her brow. 'I wasn't

the same flighty, naïve girl you'd fallen in love with by then though. My father's death changed me. The girl you knew died the moment he did. The last thing you needed was an emotionally crippled wife pulling at your attention while you were trying to build a successful future for us. You would have only resented me for it.' She frowned. 'And I loved you too much at the time to put you through all that.'

At the time.

Those three words said it all. She *had* loved him, but apparently she didn't feel the same way any more.

His chest felt hollow with sadness, the desolation of it spreading out from the centre of him, eating away at his insides.

Her voice had become increasingly shaky as she'd gone on with her speech and she stood up now and brushed a tear away from under her eye.

'Will you excuse me? I'm just going to visit the bathroom before we get back into the car,' she said, giving him a wobbly smile.

'Yes, of course,' he said, grateful for a break from the intense atmosphere so he could mull over everything she'd just told him.

He sat staring into space after she'd walked away, acutely aware of the bizarre normality of the sounds in the garden all around them while he desperately tried to make sense of the heavy weight of emotion pressing in on him.

Emma's painful confession had pierced him to the core.

He was in awe of her courage and her strength in the face of such a humbling experience, but he still couldn't shake the painful awareness that she'd chosen her mother over him.

Frustration bit at him. If she'd only let him know what was going on at the time, how bad things had got for her, he could have helped her. But she'd chosen to shut him out and handle it all without him. She hadn't trusted him or his love for her enough to let him be the husband he'd wanted to be.

Though, to be fair to her, he had to give her credit for showing such strength of character in stepping up and taking on her responsibilities, even though it had meant giving up a life with him—an easy, wrapped-in-cotton-wool existence.

If she'd been a more fragile person she could have asked him to pay off her family's debts and saddled him with a reputation for having a gold-digging wife, but she hadn't wanted that for him. Or for herself.

She had more integrity than that.

She returned a minute later and he stood up to meet her, frustration, hurt and sorrow for what they'd lost still warring in his mind.

Just as she reached the table her phone rang and she plucked it out of her bag, giving him an apologetic smile at the interruption and muttering, 'It's my mother, I'd better get this,' before answering the call.

She sounded worried at first, which made his heart thump with concern that there was more bad news to deal with, but then her voice softened into a soothing coo as she listened to a tale of woe that her mother had called to impart to her. From what he could glean from Emma's responses it sounded as if her mother's new husband, Philippe, had broken something while skiing off-piste with friends and her mother was going to have to rush back to France to see him. Emma assured her that that was fine and that she'd fly over very soon to see them both.

After cutting the call she confirmed the news, assuring him that it was better if her mother didn't hear about what was going on with them right now as she was already upset and worried about Philippe.

He wanted to say something to her about how it wasn't right for her to feel she still had to protect her mother and that it should be the other way around, but he didn't. Because it wasn't really any of his business.

For some reason that simple truth filled him with despair.

Sliding her phone back into her bag, she gave him a grateful nod for waiting and started walking back to the car. He stood rooted to the spot for a moment, watching her go, and as she reached the edge of the garden he had an over-whelming urge to try and reassure her that everything would be okay.

'Emma.'

She stopped under a large tree strung with twinkling fairy lights and turned back to face him, her expression one of open interest.

He walked quickly up to where she stood. 'I wanted to say thank you,' he said, taking another step towards her, closing more of the gap between them.

'What for?' Her brow crinkled in confusion.

'For being so honest with me just now. It's obviously still hard for you to talk about.'

She glanced away, then back at him with a small smile of gratitude.

He took another step towards her, standing so close now he could smell the intoxicating, floral scent of her.

She looked up at him, her eyes wide and bright with unshed tears.

'I also wanted to say thank you for what you did today, standing up in front of my parents like that,' he said, putting a hand on her arm, his breath hitching as he felt her tremble under his touch. 'It was brave of you.'

Glancing up, he realised there was a sprig of mistletoe hanging from a branch above them, tied in amongst the glimmering lights.

Without thinking about what he was doing, he lifted his hand and slid his fingers along her jaw, cupping her face and rubbing his thumb across the flawless skin of her cheek.

Her eyes flickered closed for a second and she drew in a small, sharp breath as if his touch had burnt her.

'Emma?' he murmured, dropping his gaze to her beautiful, Cupid's-bow-shaped mouth. A mouth that he had a sudden mad urge to kiss.

His insides felt tangled, as if she'd reached inside him and twisted them in her hands.

He wanted to do something to take away the pain and uncertainty he saw in her eyes, but intellectually he knew that kissing her now would only make things more complicated between them.

Clearly she was feeling vulnerable and there was no way he was going to consciously make that worse.

So he dropped his hand to his side and took a step away from her. Then another.

'We should get back on the road so we miss the rush-hour traffic,' he said gruffly, concerned at how wild the look in her eyes was and how flushed her cheeks were.

The stress of their situation must be getting to her too.

'Okay,' she said roughly, nodding and glancing away towards where John, their driver, stood leaning against the car, his face turned towards the late autumn sunshine.

When she looked back her eyes seemed to have taken on a glazed look.

Perhaps she was just tired.

Giving her a nod and a smile, which he hoped would go some way towards reassuring her that he was with her in this, he gestured for her to lead the way.

He watched her walk back towards the car, stumbling a little on the uneven gravel.

If they were going to get through this without getting hurt again he was going to have to be very strict with himself about how close he let himself get to her again. From this point on he would do everything in his power to make her life easier and make sure that she was as secure and happy as she deserved to be.

But he'd be doing it from a distance.

CHAPTER SEVEN

WHEN EMMA WOKE up the next morning she felt as if she hadn't slept a wink.

The memory of the way Jack had looked at her with such warmth and understanding yesterday, after she'd opened up about what she'd gone through after her father died, had haunted her dreams.

Standing under that mistletoe outside the pub, she'd thought for one heart-stopping moment that he was going to kiss her. It had actually scared her how much she'd wanted him to, but judging by his swift withdrawal apparently she'd been crazy to imagine that he'd wanted it too.

But she could have sworn...

Ugh! This was all so confusing.

She was better off on her own anyway—at

least that way she could keep full control over her life and keep her heart in one piece.

Rolling out of bed, she went over to the window and peered out at the street below, this time making sure to keep well hidden behind the curtain. There were still a few photographers lurking down on the street, but the majority of journalists seemed to have gone.

They must have grown bored with trying to get information about her. That was a relief.

After taking a quick shower and pulling on another one of the beautiful dresses that Sophie had brought over for her, this time in a flattering, draped soft green fabric that swished around her legs and clung gently to her torso, she clomped downstairs, steeling herself to face Jack again.

She had absolutely no idea what to expect from him today. What she did know was that she sure as heck wasn't going to hide from whatever was going on between them.

Walking into the kitchen, she spotted him sitting at the table with his broad back to her looking at something on his laptop.

The worry about how they were going to be with each other this morning evaporated the moment he looked round and she saw the flash of panic on his face.

'Emma, I didn't hear you come in.'

'What are you looking at?' she asked, already knowing she wasn't going to like the answer.

Snapping the laptop shut, he gave what she suspected was meant to be a diffident shrug. 'Nothing of any consequence.'

Folding her arms, she gave him a hard stare. 'Jack, there's no point in trying to hide anything from me. I'll see it sooner or later.'

He swallowed, then nodded towards the computer in front of him. 'The press found out who you are,' he said, rubbing a hand over his eyes.

Sitting down next to him, she slid the laptop towards her and opened it up to look at what he'd been reading.

All the blood seemed to drain from her head as she saw numerous links on the screen, all with her family name slashed across them with a variation on the theme of her family's money scandal and their exile from high society as well as Jack's name and title.

Gold-digger seemed to be the most commonly used term.

It was inevitable, she supposed. Once the press had that photo of her there must have been a race on to discover as much as they could about her in order to get their stories filed for this morning's news. The public seemed to be captivated by the lives of the upper-class gentry and apparently theirs were no exception.

Feeling sick, she leant back against the chair and covered her face with her hands, letting out a long low breath and concentrating hard on getting her raging heartbeat back under control.

'Are you okay?' Jack asked gently.

'I'm fine,' she said, dismissing his concern with the flip of her hand. She wasn't going to fall apart in front of him now. She still had her pride.

Getting up from the table, she smoothed her hands down her dress. 'Well, I guess if I'm going to be living here for a while I'll need to go to my flat to pick up some of my things,' she managed to say, amazed at how calm she sounded when her heart was thumping so hard she thought it might explode in her chest.

Jack looked surprised for a moment, then smiled and nodded. 'Take the car. In fact, I'll give you John's number now, then you can call him whenever you need to go somewhere.'

She frowned in surprise. 'Won't you need him?'

'I have another driver I can use.'

She must have still looked a little uncertain because he said, 'It's fine, Emma, and it's only until the press get bored and leave us alone. It'll be much less stressful for both of us.'

'Well, okay. If it's not going to cause any trouble.'

'No trouble,' he said, giving her a reassuring smile, which made something flip in her tummy.

His phone rang then, and he turned away to answer it with a curt, 'Westwood.'

She could tell from the look on his face that it wasn't someone he was keen to speak to.

He confirmed this by mouthing, 'It's Perdita,' and putting the phone on speaker so they could both hear the conversation.

'I'm calling to set up a good time to come and do that *"At home with the Earl and Countess of Redminster"* piece for the magazine,' came the journalist's crooning tones down the line.

Emma's heart sank. She'd hoped the woman would leave them alone for a little while, at least until they'd had a bit more time to practise playing the happily married couple, but apparently it was not to be.

'I was thinking a week on Friday,' Perdita continued, not giving either of them the chance to even draw breath, let alone answer. 'I'll pop over at about nine in the morning, which should mean we have plenty of light to get everything shot. Now the nights are drawing in, we have to start our days that bit earlier. Okay?' she finished finally, the uplift in her voice making the word sound more like a command than a question.

'Yes, fine,' Jack bit out. 'We'll see you then, Perdita.'

'Lovely!' Perdita breathed, then cut the call.

Jack scowled at his phone, looking as though he'd quite like to fling it across the room.

When he turned to look at her with a raised brow she matched his frustrated expression. 'So she's set on doing that interview, then,' she said, keenly aware of the tension in her voice.

'Sounds like it. We ought to do it though, just to keep my parents off our back.'

'I agree.'

He nodded. 'Thank you for understanding, Em.'

'No problem,' she said, forcing herself to smile back, feeling a little panicky about what exactly they were going to say to Perdita that would satisfy her curiosity about their relationship. They didn't even know what the state of it was themselves, for goodness' sake.

She got up from the table and went into the living room to peek out at the photographers still milling about outside.

Jack had followed her in and he flopped onto one of the sagging armchairs near the fireplace, wincing as it gave a groan of protest.

She walked over to where he sat and perched on the edge of the arm. 'You know, Perdita might think it's strange that we're living in a house like this,' she said, sweeping her hand around to encompass the nineteen seventies throwback décor. 'She'll never buy that a young couple plan to live here, and the readers certainly won't.'

He frowned. 'Good point.'

'Can you get it updated in time?' she asked hesitantly.

He ran a hand through his hair, messing up the neat waves and making her long to smooth it back down for him. 'I don't have time to arrange it right now. I'm snowed under at work.'

'I can do it,' she said before she could check herself. 'If you like,' she added less forcefully, pulling her arms tightly across her middle. 'I can't work at the moment anyway, so I may as well make myself useful.'

He looked up at her with a smile of relief. 'That would be great, if you wouldn't mind. Spend whatever you think necessary—'

She gave an involuntary grimace at that and he frowned as if realising what a tactless thing that was to say to her.

'I'll transfer some money to you to get started and if you need any more, just let me know.'

'Okay. Should I give you my account details now?' she asked, feeling incredibly awkward about discussing money with him, especially with the word *gold-digger* still floating around her mind.

'Sure. Go ahead,' he said, opening up an app on his phone and tapping in the numbers she gave him. 'I'll do a transfer as soon as I get to my desk. 'I've got a meeting in Belgravia now so I'll get out of your way.'

Emma was frustrated that they were dancing so politely around each other like this, with neither of them making any mention of their moment under the mistletoe yesterday. But then what was there to say? Nothing had actually happened.

They'd not talked at all on the journey back from Cambridge because Jack had been on the phone to his colleagues in America the whole time dealing with a crisis that had arisen, then he'd excused himself the moment they'd walked into the house, citing the need to do more work. She suspected he'd actually been avoiding having to talk about what was hanging in the air between them.

She followed him into the hallway, where Jack grabbed his coat from the cloakroom.

It can't have meant as much to him as it had to her, she decided with a sting of sadness.

It had probably just been a moment of camaraderie to him after a long and stressful day. But that was all. It hadn't meant anything more than that.

Disappointment was doing something funny

to her insides, but she squashed the feeling quickly.

'Have a good day. I'll see you later,' Jack said, sliding his arms into his overcoat and giving her a tight smile.

She nodded solemnly, not wanting to give away how disconcerted she felt about being left alone with the press still hanging around the front of the building. Not that she'd ever admit that to Jack. She didn't want him thinking he had to mollycoddle her.

'Are you sure you trust me to redecorate your house?' she blurted in a moment of nervousness, belatedly adding a twinkle of mirth to her expression so he'd see she was only joking. The idea of being let loose on this place—to have such a fun project to get immersed in—filled her with utter joy.

Flashing her a wry smile back, he leant his arm against the wall next to her and regarded her with a mock stern stare. 'If I find you've kitted the whole house out in rubber and wood-chip I will not be pleased. Other than that, go for your life. I'll be interested to see what you do with the place. It's crying out for a make over and you've always had great taste.'

'You think so?' she said, surprised by the out-of-left-field compliment.

He shot her a grin. 'You married me, didn't you?'

She couldn't stop her mouth from twisting with amusement. 'You just can't help yourself, can you?'

'I never could with you, my darling.' He leaned in a bit closer to her, capturing her gaze, and the mood changed in a second, the air seeming to crackle between them, the quiet in the hallway suddenly sounding too loud, the colours around them too bright.

Clearing his throat with a rough cough, Jack stepped back, snapping the mood, and Emma found she was digging her nails into her palms.

'I'll see you later,' he said, turning on the spot and striding away to pull the door open, then slamming it shut behind him.

The sound of him leaving reverberated around

the hallway, making her suddenly feel very, very alone in the big empty house.

It took Emma a good twenty minutes to come down from her jittery high after Jack left.

Crikey, it was going to be hard, living here with him and having to get through those moments when they both became uncomfortably aware of how happy they'd once been together, but how much had come between them since.

Despite her body telling her she wanted him, more desperately than she could believe, she knew deep down that hoping things would get physical between them was foolish when their feelings about each other were so tangled. It would only make living together more problematic than it already was.

Sighing, she made her way to the kitchen to put the kettle on for a much-needed cup of tea.

At least throwing herself into redecorating the house would give her something to distract herself from thinking about him all the time.

Her thoughts were interrupted by the sound

of her phone ringing in her back pocket. Plucking it out, she was pleased to see Grace's name flash up on the screen.

'Hello, you, how's it going?'

'I was going to ask you the same thing. I hope you don't mind, but Sophie filled me in on what happened after Jolyon's party and I read about the rest of it in the papers. Nice photo of you and your husband on the *Babbler* website by the way.'

'Er—thanks.' Was the picture out already? She hadn't expected it to appear for another few days. Thank goodness her mother never looked at the internet and was unlikely to see any of the news articles over in France.

'Are you okay, Emma? You must be having a rough time with the press camped out on your doorstep,' Grace asked in her usual no-nonsense manner.

There was a long pause where Emma tried to form a coherent sentence about how she felt about it all.

Where to begin?

'Yes, I'm fine. It all feels like a dream, to be honest, but we're handling it.'

'So you really are married to an earl?' There was a note of gleeful fascination in her friend's voice now.

'I am.' She swallowed, feeling her earlier nervousness returning. 'Although for how much longer I don't know,' she blurted.

There was a pause on the line. 'Really? Are things difficult between you?'

Emma sighed, annoyed with herself for losing her cool like that. She didn't want Grace to worry about her; her friend had enough on her plate. 'No, no, it's fine, ignore me. I'm just a bit stressed at the minute. I'm supposed to be interior designing the downstairs of the house we're living in for a photo shoot a week on Friday and I have absolutely no idea where to start.'

There was another small pause on the line before Grace spoke again. 'You know, I worked in a lovely boutique hotel in Chelsea called Daphne's a while ago. It has every bedroom decorated in a style from a different time period and the communal rooms are done out in a really cool and quirky way. It would be a great place to get some inspiration.'

'Ooh, I think I know it,' Emma said, feeling excitement begin to bubble in her stomach. 'I read an article about it a while ago. I've been meaning to go and have a peek at it. It looked like a fascinating place.'

'You should,' Grace said. 'I'm sure the manager would jump at the chance to show you around if you suggested that you were thinking about hiring the place for your vow-renewal ceremony.'

Emma tried to ignore the twist of unease that the mention of renewing their vows provoked.

'It would be great publicity for them if they could boast about having the famous Earl and Countess of Redminster as patrons,' Grace added with a smile in her voice.

'That's a fantastic idea,' Emma said, feeling a real buzz of excitement now. It was exactly what she needed today: a chance to escape from the house and take her mind off Jack for a while.

'I don't suppose you're free today to come with me, are you?' she asked her friend. 'We could go for a coffee afterwards.'

It would be lovely to spend some time in Grace's easy company. She desperately needed to do something *normal* feeling after the craziness of the last couple of days.

'I'd love to,' Grace said. 'I've just finished work so I can meet you there in half an hour.'

'Fantastic,' Emma said with a grateful sigh. 'I'll see you there.'

They spent a happy half-hour looking around the hotel, with Emma making copious notes on things that inspired her, then chatting it all over with Grace over large mugs of cream-topped hot chocolate in a nearby café afterwards, sitting next to a large Scandinavian-style Christmas tree hung with silvery white snowflakes, quirky wooden reindeer and red felt hearts.

It was lovely spending time with just Grace on her own for once and they discovered to their delight just how much their tastes aligned. It turned out Grace wasn't a fan of the pure white and chrome interior look that Emma had teased Jack about either.

'That must be tough,' she said, as her friend finished a diatribe about the hotel where she was currently working, which felt so clinical she was continually transported back to the months she'd spent visiting her grandmother in hospital before cancer finally took her from her.

'Your house is going to look wonderful when you're finished,' Grace said, changing the subject and shaking off the air of sadness that had fallen over her at the mention of her beloved grandmother—the woman, Emma knew, who had been more like a mother to Grace.

She was perpetually impressed by the strength and tenacity that Grace showed to the world, despite having had such a tough start in life.

'What a fantastic opportunity to showcase your skills as a designer too,' her friend said. 'Hey, do you think it's something you'd be interested in pursuing as a career?'

Giving Grace a smile, she shrugged non-committally, but felt a tug of something akin to excitement deep in her belly. She'd always loved art and design at school and had done both a graphic design and business night class recently in the hope she'd be able to apply her artistic bent to a job in the future. Fortuitously, the classes had given her a set of skills to be able to make up mood boards on a computer, put together cost sheets and even do some technical drawing, which would no doubt prove very useful for this project.

While she'd been paying off her father's debts she hadn't allowed herself to think about what else she could be doing with her life, but now she was getting so close to reconciling them it really was time to think about the next steps. As much as she loved working for Clio at the Maids in Chelsea agency, she'd be very happy for her long-term career to take another direction. One that didn't involve toadying to people who made an art form of peering down their noses at the hired help. She'd probably have to go to college and get proper qualifications if she wanted to pursue something like interior design, which she'd need to save up for, but it was a worthy goal to aim for.

It would be a good way to safeguard a more settled future for herself.

After losing everything she had once already, she never wanted to be in a position where she was at risk of that happening again. No way was she going to rely on someone else to keep her afloat.

Pushing away a concern about how this fed into her muddled feelings regarding her relationship with Jack, she turned her attention back to her friend.

'Thanks so much for today, Grace, it's been really useful. Now all I have to do is get out there and make it happen.'

CHAPTER EIGHT

To HER DISAPPOINTMENT, Emma didn't see much of Jack over the next ten days. For the first couple of them his work took him into his office in the City at a totally unreasonable hour in the morning and kept him there until well after Emma had dragged herself to bed in the evenings. Though to be fair, she *was* crashing out early after long, intense days of researching and planning the new design scheme for the downstairs of the house.

On the odd occasion when she did see him their conversations were stilted and tended to focus on the practicalities of living together, with him excusing himself before she had chance to ask him anything of a personal nature.

Seeing the place in total disarray on Friday

night when he returned from work, Jack had then suddenly announced he was flying off to Italy for a few days to meet with a business acquaintance, though she suspected he was deliberately making himself scarce—partly to avoid having to live in what felt very much like a building site, but mostly to avoid having to be around her all weekend.

This thought made her stomach twist with a mixture of sadness and dejection. She'd really hoped that her confession in the pub garden would bring them closer, but instead it seemed to have driven even more of a wedge between them, crushing any hope she'd once had of a reconciliation.

So it was actually a relief in a way to have this huge project to take her mind off things.

With the contacts that she and her friends from the agency had managed to scrape together between them, she'd hired a talented, hard-working team and less than two weeks on she barely recognised the place. Luckily it had only needed cosmetic changes—though old, the house had been kept in good condition—and they'd been achieved with the minimum of fuss.

She'd not had so much fun at work in a very long time.

The new furniture was sourced from a couple of funky little independent shops on Columbia Road, which suited the brighter, more contemporary palette of colours she'd chosen for the walls and flooring. While it wasn't up to Daphne's standards of wow factor, she was delighted with the end result.

It was a much more relaxing, comfortable place to hang out in now.

When Jack returned a couple of days before they were due to do the interview with Perdita she stood nervously in the living room with him, crossing her fingers as he stared around him with an expression of pure amazement on his face.

'Well, Em, I think you've found your calling. This is fantastic!' he said finally, turning to give her a wide, genuine smile.

Her heart lurched at the sight of his pleasure, the tension in her shoulders fading away.

'Not a woodchip to be seen,' she joked, feeling her tummy flip when he grinned back at her.

'You've done an amazing job, thank you,' he said, walking over to where she stood.

Seeing him here again, with his hair dishevelled and dark smudges under his eyes, had sent her senses into overdrive and she was having a hard time keeping her nerves under wraps.

'I'm glad you like it. I had a real blast working on it,' she said, having to force herself to maintain eye contact so he wouldn't see how jittery she was feeling in his charismatic presence.

'I can tell. It shows,' he said, looking at her with a strange expression now. Was that pride she could see in his eyes?

Prickly heat rushed over her skin as they both stared at each other for a long, tension-filled moment.

Jack broke the atmosphere by clearing his throat. 'Well, I'm going to go and check in with the US office then head off to bed,' he said, running a hand over his tousled hair. He looked so exhausted she had a mad urge to spring into full-on wife mode and start fussing around him, telling him not to bother with work, but to go straight to bed and get some rest.

She didn't though.

Because she knew that it wasn't her place to do that. She was only his wife in name after all.

Sadness swamped her as she accepted the painful reality that she'd forfeited the right to have a say in how he lived his life six years ago.

He wasn't hers to care for any more.

The next morning, just one day before Perdita and her crew were due to sweep in and dissect their lives for the entertainment of the general public like some kind of twisted anthropology project, she was surprised to see Jack striding into the kitchen at nine o'clock in the morning.

She was in the process of stuffing her mouth with a croissant she'd rewarded herself with for all her hard work over the last few days, so it

took her a moment to comment on his remark-
able appearance.

'What are you doing here?' she muttered
through a mouthful of buttery pastry, her heart
racing at the sight of him looking all fresh and
clean from the shower and, oh, so strikingly
handsome in a dark grey, sharply tailored Italian suit.

'I happen to live here,' he replied, with one
eyebrow raised.

'I know that. I'm just surprised to see you here
so late in the day. You've always been up and
out with the lark before now.'

'Some of us don't have the good fortune of
having regular lie-ins,' he said, the twinkle in
his eye letting her know he was only teasing
her.

She turned back to her plate and chewed the
last of the croissant hard, feeling heat rise to
her cheeks. She hadn't even brushed her hair
this morning and was still in her scruffy old
brushed-cotton pyjamas, assuming he'd already

left for the office when she'd got up to a quiet house.

Hearing the kettle begin to boil, she turned to look towards where he now stood, dropping a teabag into a mug. The ends of his hair were curling around the collar of his pristine white shirt and without thinking she said, 'You need a haircut.'

Swivelling to face her, he shot her an amused grin. 'Are you nagging me, wife?'

The heat in her cheeks increased. 'No!' She cleared her throat, distracted by the sudden lump she found there. 'I don't know why I said that. I just noticed, that's all.'

Turning back to her croissant again, she tried to ignore his rueful chuckle and the clinking and clanking noises as he made his breakfast. Grace and economy of movement had never been his more dominant traits.

He sat down opposite her, bringing with him his fresh, clean scent, and her stomach did a little dance.

Trying to smooth out some of the tangles in her hair, she gave him a sheepish smile.

Not that she should worry about what Jack thought of her looking such a mess. He'd always liked seeing her in disarray and had often commented on how sexy he found it after they'd made love in the good old days.

The rogue memory of it only made her face flame even hotter.

'How come you're not in the office already?' she asked, concentrating on brushing her fingers together to knock off the remaining flaky crumbs so she didn't have to look him in the eye.

'I have a meeting in Chelsea at nine-thirty so I'm having a slow start to the morning for once.' He shifted in his chair so he could pick up his mug of tea and take a swig from it, peering at her from over the top of the rim.

'And I have a favour to ask of you,' he said, once he'd had a good swallow of tea.

She looked at him in surprise. 'A favour?'

'Yes.'

'What is it?'

He shifted in his chair again, only this time looking a little discomfited.

'We've been invited to a party tonight, by a business acquaintance of mine. I could do with turning up and doing some schmoozing. The guy might be interested in having me buy out his company and I wanted to work on him in a more relaxed environment.'

'Okay,' she said slowly, her pulse picking up at the thought of spending the evening at his side. 'This is tonight, did you say?'

'Yes. It's in a house a couple of streets away.'

'And you want me to go with you as your *wife*?' Saying the words made her ache a little inside.

'You've got it in one.' He flashed her a grin, which she struggled to return.

Splaying his hands on the table, he looked her directly in the eye now. 'Look, I know it's probably the last thing you feel like doing, what with our lives and relationship being so complicated at the moment, but I wouldn't ask if it wasn't really important.'

She glanced down at the table where his hands still lay spread on the solid oak top, her eyes snagging on the second finger of his left hand as she noticed something glinting there.

He was wearing his wedding ring.

Her blood began to pound through her veins. Even though she knew it was all for show, the sight of the gold ring that she'd touched with such wonder and awe after she'd slid it onto his finger at their simple wedding ceremony, back there on his finger, made her body buzz with elation.

'Yes, okay, I'll go,' she blurted, buoyed by the fact that he'd asked for her help. She would happily do whatever it took to make things easier between them. She owed him that. And she'd missed him while he'd been away and liked the idea of spending time with him this evening.

His look of gratified surprise made her think he'd been expecting her to refuse.

'Thank you, Emma, I really appreciate it.'

'You're welcome.'

His full mouth widened into a smile, the lines at the corners of his eyes deepening, reviving the look of boyish charm that had swept her off her feet all those years ago, stealing her breath away.

She loved his face, especially when he let down that façade of cool that he wore for the rest of the world. It had taken a long time for him to trust her enough to let her see the real him, but when he had it had blown her away.

Was this the Jack she used to know finally peering out at her?

They stared at each other for another long, painful moment, where her traitorous brain decided to give her a Technicolor recap of the most blissful moments from their past, until she finally managed to tear her gaze away from his and stand up.

'What time do we need to get there?' she asked, making a big show of pushing her chair neatly under the table so she didn't have to look at him again in case her apprehension was written all over her face. She needed to remember that this was just a business arrangement to him, not a date.

'We'll leave here at eight-thirty. It's a formal do, so if you have a little black dress or something it would be great if you could wear it.'

His voice sounded strained now and she wondered wistfully whether she'd somehow infected him with her own feelings of poignant nostalgia.

'No problem,' she said, turning and walking away from him before she blurted out something she might regret later.

The party was in full swing when they arrived and Emma was surprised, but delighted, when Jack kept hold of her arm after helping her climb the smooth slate steps up to the house in her sky-high heels. He'd been very complimentary about how she looked this evening, and she'd had to forcefully remind herself that his noticing how she looked probably didn't mean the same thing to him as it did to her.

After greeting their hosts, they walked into the living room to mingle with the rest of the partygoers and he turned to give her a reassuring smile as she tightened her grip on him, feeling a little overawed at being a guest at a party like this again.

'Just relax, it's a friendly crowd,' he told her.

But unfortunately he couldn't have been more wrong.

'Oh, no!' she whispered, coming to a halt in the middle of the room as a horrible thump of recognition hit her in the chest at the sight of a group of people standing next to the large picture window.

Angry resentment rattled through her as she relived the whispered taunts and cruel asides she'd been the victim to from this very group of people after the scandalous news about her father came out.

'Vultures,' she whispered to Jack, 'who used to call themselves friends of my family, until they called in their loans and sold us out to the press.'

Looking up into his handsome face, she was a little afraid of what she might see there. Would he be sorry now that he'd brought her here to-night?

But instead of showing concern, his eyes darkened with anger. 'No one here will dare say a word to you, I promise you that,' he growled, putting her in mind of a wild animal defending its territory. 'If anyone so much as smirks in your general direction I'll make sure they regret it.'

Her heart leapt at his show of protectiveness, but she knew she couldn't really expect him to step in for her; this was her problem to deal with, not his. 'As heartening as this display of macho chest-beating is, I can't expect you to hang around by my side all night, ready to jump in and defend my honour,' she joked, trying to lighten the atmosphere. She didn't want this to have any kind of impact on his business deal.

'Yes, you can, Em. You're my wife and I'm staying right here next to you.'

The resolve in his eyes gave her goose bumps.

She knew he meant every word he said—could feel it in the crackling atmosphere around him. He would look after her tonight, if she needed him to.

'Emma, look at me,' he said quietly, cupping her jaw in his hands and drawing her closer to him so she was forced to look him in the eye, her pulse playing a merry beat in her throat.

'You're the bravest person I know,' he said. 'You didn't slink away and give up when everything went to hell for you and I know you won't give these idiots the satisfaction of breaking you tonight either. This is an opportunity for you to show them just how incredibly strong you are and how much you've achieved despite the cards being stacked against you. You should be proud of yourself. I'm proud of you. Proud to call you my wife.'

The air beat a pulse between them, as she rolled his pep talk around in her mind. He was proud of her? Proud to be her husband? Hearing those words suddenly made her anger at the people here fade into the background. She could handle anything they said to her if she truly had Jack on her side. There wasn't anything they could do to hurt her any more.

Buoyed by that uplifting insight, she gave Jack a grateful nod and a smile.

'It means a lot to me to hear you say that, Jack.' She turned and took his arm again, wrapping her fingers tightly around his biceps, feeling him pull her more tightly against his body.

To her surprise, Jack then marched them straight up to the group, who were staring at them with a kind of cynical fascination.

'Do you have something you'd like to say to my wife?' Jack growled at them and she was both astonished and amused to see them all take a small step backwards and shake their heads as one.

'We were just saying what an impressive couple you make,' a red-faced man who used to go out shooting with her father said in a faltering voice. 'And that you're a very lucky man to have such a beautiful wife, Westwood.'

The whole group nodded in agreement, but

Jack didn't move away from them, giving every last one of them that unnerving weighted stare that Emma knew from first-hand experience he was so good at employing.

'And that we're sorry we weren't more supportive about your situation after your father died, Emma,' a tall, moustached man with a slight stoop said hurriedly. 'It's good to see that you're happy and settled now though,' he added.

Emma coolly nodded her thanks, knowing he didn't mean a word of it.

Not that she cared one jot.

'It's all water under the bridge,' she said, smiling serenely to show them just how little they meant to her now.

After that, they strode confidently around the room, arm in arm in a show of solidarity, with Jack loudly and proudly introducing her to everyone as his wife, and her floating around on a cloud of happy contentment.

Jack's gaze followed Emma as she walked back towards him after getting her glass refilled at the makeshift bar that Rob, a prospective business partner, had set up in the corner of his grand living room.

She really was breathtaking to behold. Her head was held high and her body language confident, showcasing the natural elegance and poise he admired so much in her.

Emma had been brilliant with Rob, laughing at his jokes and showing interest in his tales of his children and their schooling. She'd asked him intelligent questions and had clearly listened to the answers because she was able to comment on them with thoughtful insight. Even Rob's wife was charmed by her, which was an unexpected bonus. The woman was known for being standoffish with the wives of her husband's business acquaintances, but Emma had managed to break through her wall of cool and engage her in a conversation about interior design and the woman had even gone so far as to give Emma a quick tour of their newly decorated bedrooms.

He'd been intrigued to see how genuinely interested Emma was in talking about the redecoration she'd done to his house. Considering how little time she'd had to get it done, he was hugely impressed by what she'd achieved. And she really seemed to have enjoyed it too, judging by the gleam in her eye and the flush in her cheeks when they'd looked over the improvements together.

It seemed she was a natural.

And far too talented to be wasting her time serving drinks at parties.

He ran a hand over his hair, watching with a growing sense of impatience as she stopped to talk to a woman who pointed at the dress she was wearing and gave her a complimentary smile.

Even though he'd been flat out with work, he'd not been able to keep his mind off the knowledge that she'd be there in his house when he got home each evening—and, even more frustratingly, that he wouldn't be returning to one of her beguiling smiles and her soothing embrace.

After having time away from her for the last

week or so, which had given him more of a chance to ruminate on what she'd revealed after they'd visited his parents' house, he realised that her heartfelt admission seemed to have broken the evil spell his pride had held over him since they'd parted ways.

He ached to be on friendlier terms with her, rather than having to step so carefully around her as he had been doing.

Hopefully the plan he'd put in place for when they were finally able to escape this party would set him on a path towards that.

'Did you manage to speak to Rob alone? Is it a done deal?' Emma murmured into his ear as she finally made it back to where he stood.

The soft caress of her breath on his skin chased shivers up his spine.

Taking a steadying breath, he turned to look her in the eye; hyperaware of his pulse beating an erratic rhythm through his veins as he looked into her beautiful face and saw only genuine interest and concern for him there.

Was there still something there between them?

And could there be something again, even after all this time?

He pushed the thought away, knowing he was playing with fire even considering the idea.

'Yes, I'm all done here. It's time to go,' he told her, detecting a flash of relief on her face.

He made a mental note to pay her back tenfold for putting herself out for him like this. Her willingness to help him proved she was still the same big-hearted, generous person she'd always been. This travesty with her father hadn't broken her—in fact, like the age-old adage, it had only made her stronger.

Taking her hand, he gently led her towards the door, where their hosts were standing, chatting to a group of new people that had just arrived.

'Rob, we're going to make a move. Thanks for a good party,' he said to his future associate, shaking the man's hand.

'Glad the two of you could make it,' Rob said, returning the firm handshake and giving Emma a courteous nod. 'It was lovely to meet you,

Emma. I hope we get to spend more time with you soon.'

He meant it too; Jack could tell by the conviction in the man's voice. It was one of the things that had him excited about amalgamating their companies. Rob was well known for his straight-talking attitude and ability to cut through the bull. They seemed to be very similar in the way they conducted business and he was going to be a most useful ally.

'Thank you for your kind hospitality,' Emma said graciously, returning Rob's smile and accepting a kiss on both cheeks from his apparently rather lovestruck wife, who was gazing at Emma with something akin to adoration in her eyes.

Not that he was surprised; she was such a genuine, warm person it was impossible not to fall under her spell.

The air was mercifully cool on his overheated skin as they walked carefully down the smooth slate steps of the Chelsea town house, making allowances for Emma's high heels.

His body twitched with nerves as he ran over what he had planned for them this evening. It had taken some doing—calling in favours from here, there and everywhere—but he was pleased with what he'd been able to pull together at the last second.

The idea had struck him earlier as he'd watched her walk away from the kitchen table looking adorably dishevelled in her baggy old pyjamas that had done absolutely nothing to dampen his body's desire for her.

She was the kind of woman that would look sexy in a hessian sack.

After the years of hard work she'd put into clearing her father's name, denying herself the kind of life that she ought to have been living as a young, driven and intelligent woman, it was time she was allowed to have some fun for once.

As they reached the pavement, right on cue his driver pulled up next to them in the car.

Emma turned to frown at him. 'You ordered the car to pick us up to drive us the two streets home? I know my heels are a bit high, but I think that's what you'd call overkill, Jack. I can make it a hundred yards in them without falling flat on my face, you know.'

He shot her a grin. 'I'm sure you can, but do you really want to take the chance? Especially if we have to make a run for it into the house.'

Shaking her long, sleek hair back over her shoulder, she gave an indifferent shrug. 'I've been managing fine all evening and I'm getting quite good at putting on a blithely bored face for any journos that cross my path now.'

He smiled as she treated him to a demonstration of the facial expression she'd just described.

'Actually, we're not going home,' he told her.

'Where are we going, then? We have the interview with Perdita in the morning, remember, and I don't think she'll be too impressed to have to change her article's name to *"At home with two hungover zombies"*. It's not that kind of magazine.'

Flashing her a grin of wry amusement, he

motioned for her to get into the car, holding the door open for her and raising a playful eyebrow when she frowned at him in confusion.

'Don't worry, Cinderella, I'll have you back before midnight. Well, maybe a *little* after midnight.'

'From *where*?' she asked pointedly.

'You'll see. It's a surprise. Trust me,' he added when she gave him the side-eye.

Muttering under her breath, she finally relented and slid into the back seat of the car, swinging her long legs in last so he was rewarded with a flash of her slender, creamy-skinned thighs before shutting the door for her.

The evocative image remained stubbornly planted in his mind until he managed to shake it out by determinedly replacing it with a vision of his plan for the evening.

The car drove them slowly out of Chelsea then along the tree-lined Embankment that ran next to the majestic expanse of the river Thames, the newly hung sparkling Christmas lights running parallel with their route. Taking a right, they travelled across Vauxhall Bridge then past the vibrant greenery of Lambeth Palace Gardens until their final destination was in sight.

Emma didn't utter a word throughout their whole journey, but repeatedly gave him search-ing looks as famous landmarks passed them by, which he gently rebuffed each time with a secretive smile.

By the time John pulled the car up a short walking distance from the South Bank prom-enade her brow was so crinkled and her eyes so wide with bafflement he couldn't help but laugh.

'We're here,' he said, and, not waiting for her reply, he got out to walk round the back of the car and open her door for her. 'I wanted to do something to say thank you for all the work you've put into making the house look so spec-tacular,' he said as he took her hand and helped her out of the car, holding onto her until she'd centred her balance on those preposterously high heels of hers.

Her fingers felt cool and fragile in his grip and he had a mad urge to wrap his arms around her and hold her close, to let her know he was there for her now and she didn't need to do it on her own any more.

He didn't though, afraid that he might wind up with both a sore shin and a profoundly bruised ego.

Not that he didn't deserve that.

'Are we going to see a film?' she asked with a hint of disappointment in her voice.

'Nope,' he said, looping his arm through hers and letting out a secret breath of relief when she didn't pull away from him.

Her body radiated heat next to him as they walked along the mercifully deserted riverside towards their destination, arm in arm, the culmination of his plan for the evening looming over them in all its grand spherical glory.

She stumbled a little and he tightened his grip to keep her upright.

'Okay, you're going to have to tell me where we're going so I know how far I have to make it in these *not made for hiking along the South Bank* heels,' she grumbled.

He smiled at her frustration, which of course only made her scowl back at him.

'Okay, we're here,' he said as they reached the entrance to the London Eye where a young woman was standing at the end of a plush red carpet, snuggled into a jacket branded with the attraction's logo.

Emma stared at him in surprise. 'The Eye? But I thought they closed it at night.'

'Not for us. They've made a special exception.'

She blinked twice. 'Why?'

'Because when I told them how much you deserved a chance to finally have something you wanted they had no choice but to say yes.'

She looked at him as if she couldn't quite believe this was happening, her nose adorably wrinkled.

'Let's get on,' he said, tugging gently on her arm.

She looked up at him and he smiled at the expression of awe on her face.

'I hope you're ready for the ride of your life, Em.'

CHAPTER NINE

EMMA SMILED IN stunned wonder at the woman who greeted them warmly by name and invited them to board one of the luxurious glass-domed pods that gradually travelled upwards to give the rider an unsurpassed view of the London skyline.

Tightening his grip on her arm, as if sensing she needed a little persuading to believe this was actually real, Jack guided her along the carpet and into the dimly lit interior of the pod, where the doors immediately swished closed behind them.

It hit her then exactly what this meant.

Jack had remembered how she'd once talked about wanting to commandeer the whole wheel for her own personal ride one day, so she could look down on the sprawling metropolis at midnight—how it was on her whimsical bucket list to gaze down at the city that had always held such excitement for her in her youth and feel like a goddess of all she surveyed.

He'd remembered that and gone out of his way to make it happen for her.

Her heart did a somersault in her chest at the thought.

In fact the only thing missing from her fantasy was—

'Champagne!'

Swivelling to face him, she was totally unable to keep the astonished grin off her face. 'You arranged for a bottle of champagne on ice for us to drink up there?'

'I did.' The look of deep gratification in his eyes at her excited response sent shivers down her spine.

Deftly popping the cork out of the bottle, he filled two flutes and handed one to her.

She took it with a trembling hand, first clinking it against his then taking a long sip in the hope the alcohol would help calm her raging pulse.

'Cheers,' he murmured, taking a sip from his own glass but keeping his gaze fixed firmly on hers.

Unable to maintain eye contact for fear of giving away her nervous excitement at what he'd done for her and what it could mean, she moved away from him, taking a long, low breath in an attempt to pull herself together. She shouldn't read too much into this. After all, he'd made sure to tell her it was a reward for helping him out, nothing more.

Walking further into the pod and taking another large gulp of fizz, she noticed that the large wooden bench in the middle had been covered in soft red velvet cushions for them to sit on.

'You know, for the want of a camping stove and some basic provisions I could probably live in here for the rest of my life,' she joked nervously, walking over to look out of the floor-to-ceiling glass windows as the pod continued its breathtaking ascent.

The hairs stood up on the back of her neck as she felt him come to stand behind her, so close that she could feel his warm breath tickling the skin of her cheek.

'Beautiful,' he murmured, and she wasn't sure whether he was talking about her or the view.

She was trembling all over now, unable to keep her nerves at being here alone with him from visibly showing. It *terrified* her how much she craved to feel his arms around her, holding her tightly as they enjoyed this experience together.

Taking another big gulp of champagne, she was surprised to find she'd finished the glassful.

'Here, let me refill that for you,' Jack said, taking the flute gently out of her fingers.

She stared sightlessly out at the view, her senses entirely diverted by the man moving purposefully around behind her.

He returned a moment later and she took the refilled glass gratefully from him, recognising a desperate need to maintain the bolstering buzz of courage that the alcohol gave her as it warmed her chest.

'Em? Are you okay?' she heard him murmur behind her, the power of his presence overwhelming her senses and making her head spin.

'I'm fine, Jack.'

He put a hand on her arm, urging her to turn and face him.

Swivelling reluctantly on the spot, she looked up into his captivating eyes.

'You were amazing tonight, you know,' he said, pushing a strand of hair away from her face and tucking it behind her ear, sending a rush of goose bumps across her skin where he touched her. 'You conducted yourself with such integrity, a quality a lot of the people there tonight would never be able to claim for themselves.'

'Thank you.' Her words came out sounding stilted and coarse due to a sudden constriction in her chest. 'Well, I'm glad I didn't let you down as your—' she swallowed '—wife.'

He snorted gently and glanced down, frowning. 'You've never let me down, Em.' When he looked back at her his eyes were full of regret. 'It was me that expected too much from you too fast after your father died, then gave up on you too quickly. I've been selfish and short-sighted.'

She blinked, shocked by his sudden confession and not sure how to respond to it.

He sighed, his shoulders slumping. Moving to stand next to her now at the floor-to-ceiling window, he rested his forehead against the glass and stared out across the vast, night-lit city. They were a good way up in the air now, much higher than any of the buildings that surrounded them.

Together, but alone, at the top of the world.

'I hate myself for the way I treated you back then. I don't know what made me think it was okay to expect you to jump, just because I asked you to. I was an arrogant, naïve fool who had no idea how a marriage really worked.'

Pushing away from the window, he turned to face her again, his expression fierce.

'I miss what we had, Emma.'

He took a small step towards her and her heart rate accelerated.

'I remember everything from our time together as if it was yesterday,' he murmured, his gaze sweeping her face. 'How beautiful you look when you wake up all tousled in the mornings, the way your laugh never fails to send a shiver down my spine, how kind and non-judgemental you are towards every single person you meet.' His gaze rested on her mouth, which tingled in response to his avid attention.

'You're a good person through and through, Emma Westwood.'

Adrenaline was making her heart leap about in her chest now and the pod, which had felt so spacious for two people only minutes ago, suddenly felt too small.

His dark gaze moved up to fix on hers. 'I've been punishing you for rejecting me—' he took a ragged breath '—because you broke my heart, Em.' His voice cracked on the words and on instinct she reached out to lay a hand against his chest, over his heart, as if she could somehow undo the damage she'd done to it.

He glanced down at where her hand lay before looking up to recapture her gaze with his. 'The way I responded was totally unfair. I know that now. And I'm sorry. Truly sorry, Emma.'

Her breath caught in her throat as she saw tears well in his eyes.

He was hurting as badly as she was.

This revelation finally broke through her restraint and an overwhelming urge to soothe him compelled her to close the gap between them. Wrapping her arms around him, she pressed her lips to his and immediately felt him respond by pulling her hard against his body and kissing her back with an intensity that took her breath away.

Opening her mouth to drag in a gasp of pleasure, she felt his tongue slide between her parted lips and skim against her own, bringing with it the heady familiar taste of him. She'd missed kissing him, so profoundly it made her physically ache with relief to finally be able to revel in its glorious return.

They moved against each other in an exquisitely sensual dance, their hands pushing under clothing, sliding over skin, reading each other's bodies with their fingertips.

Stumbling together, they moved to the centre of the pod and Jack carefully laid her down on the soft velvet cushions, not letting her go for a second, and she let him take control, forcing herself not to ruin this by questioning the wisdom of what they were doing—because she needed this right now, needed to blot out all the complications and responsibilities in her life and just sink into the safe familiarity of his strength.

To feel desired and happy and free again.

The sex was fast and desperate, as if they couldn't stop themselves even if they'd wanted to. Their hands and mouths were everywhere, their touch wild and unrestrained.

Alone, but together, at the top of the world.

* * *

Afterwards, after they'd come back down to earth and stumbled out of the pod, rumpled and high on champagne and emotion, they returned home and made love again, this time taking the opportunity to explore each other's bodies properly, relearning what they used to know and finding comfort and joy in the fact that being together again was as wonderful as they remembered—maybe even more so—until they finally fell asleep in each other's arms, both mentally and physically replete after their long-awaited wedding night.

Jack woke the next morning with a deep sense of satisfaction warming his body.

Memories of having Emma in his arms last night swam across his vision and he allowed himself to exult in them for a while before opening his eyes.

He hadn't intended to make love to her last night, the trip on the London Eye was meant to be an apology for the awful, cold way he'd been acting towards her, but she'd looked so wary to be there alone with him he'd known if he wanted to gain her trust again he was going to have to be totally honest with her about how he was feeling.

It had been incredibly hard saying those things to her after years of burying his feelings so deeply inside him, but he was intensely relieved that they were finally out in the open.

He knew now with agonising certainty that he'd never felt like this with anyone but her. The women he'd dated in the years they'd been apart had all been pale imitations of her. Mere tracing paper versions. Without substance. None of them had her grace and finesse, or her smart, sharp wit. Or her beauty.

After Emma had left him, he'd shut himself off from romantic emotion, not wanting to deal with the torment he'd been put through, but as soon as she'd reappeared in his life all those feelings had come rushing back. But it had been too painful to bear at first, like emotional pins and needles. So he'd numbed himself against her.

Until it wasn't possible to any more.

From the way she'd kept herself gently aloof from him since they'd met again he'd been afraid that she wasn't interested in renewing their connection—that she'd moved on from him—but judging by the passionate fervour of her lovemaking last night, it seemed she did still care about him after all.

Which led him to believe that there might be hope for them yet.

Excitement buzzed through his veins and he turned to look for the woman who had made him an intensely happy man last night, only to be disappointed when he found the space where she'd lain in bed next to him empty and cold.

Frowning, he grabbed his phone, glancing at the screen to see it was already eight-thirty. It wasn't like him to sleep in late, but after the intensity of the night before he guessed it wasn't entirely surprising.

At least he'd taken today off work to be available for the *Babbler* interview, so he and Emma would be able to spend the day in each other's company—hopefully most of it in bed.

Heart feeling lighter than it had in years, he got up and took a quick shower, then pulled on some fresh clothes.

It was a shame there wasn't time to lure her back to bed now. That damn interview! It was the very last thing he wanted to do today.

Still, perhaps once Perdita had cleared off he could take Emma out for a slap-up meal to apologise for forcing her to take part in his father's media circus, then drag her back to the house for a lot more personal attention and a chance for them to talk about their future together.

Taking the stairs two at a time, he went straight to the kitchen to seek out Emma so they could start their life together again as soon as possible.

Emma had woken up in the dark to find Jack's arm lying heavily across her chest and his leg hooked over hers, trapping her within the cage of his body.

Her first thought was, *What have I done?*

She'd let her crazy romantic notions get the better of her, that was what.

She was suddenly terrified that she'd made a terrible mistake.

Heart pounding, she'd wriggled out of his covetous embrace and dashed into the en-suite bathroom, her forehead damp with sweat and her limbs twitchy with adrenaline.

After splashing some water on her face and feeling her heart rate begin to return to normal, she'd crept back out to the bedroom and stood looking at Jack as he slept. He'd looked so peaceful, lying there on his side, with his arm still outstretched as if he were holding onto the ghost of her presence.

Unable to bear the idea of getting back into bed with him when her feelings were in such chaos, she went to her own room to get dressed, then headed downstairs to make herself a soothing cup of tea. She sat with it at the table, staring into space and thinking, thinking, thinking...

Half an hour later, she was still sitting there with a cold cup of tea in front of her, her thoughts a blur of conflicting emotions.

She was so confused, so twisted into knots. In her haze of lust and alcohol last night she'd thought she'd be able to remain in control and keep her feelings safe.

What an idiot she'd been.

It hadn't taken much for him to break through the barriers she'd so carefully constructed over the last six years to keep her safe from any more emotional upheaval.

Just the thought of it made her go cold with fear.

What had she been thinking, imagining rec-onciliation with Jack was what she wanted? It was crazy to try and reinstate what they'd once had. Impossible! They couldn't just pick up where they'd left off and she couldn't put her-self through the torment of wondering when it was all going to be ripped away from her again.

Because it would be.

She didn't get to keep the people she loved.

Anyway, he was still probably clinging on to a vision of her from when she was eighteen, all bright-eyed and full of naïve optimism. The Emma she'd been then was the perfect match for someone of his standing—a billionaire businessman and earl of the realm—but the Emma she was now was all wrong to be the wife of someone like that. Especially as his family put such store in appearances. They'd humoured the match up till now, but surely it would cause all sorts of friction for Jack in the future. It could tear his family apart, and, after having her own torn asunder, that was the last thing she'd wish on him.

He'd only end up hating her for it.

After already suffering through the turmoil of losing him once; she couldn't bear the thought of going through it again. It would break her in two.

She jumped in surprise as Jack came striding

into the kitchen looking all rumpled and sexy, with a wide smile on his face.

Her stomach did an almighty flip at the sight of him, but she dug her fingernails into the table top, reminding herself of all the reasons why it would be a bad idea to take things any further with him.

Striding over to where she sat, he bent down to kiss her and she steeled herself, flinching a little as his mouth made contact with hers.

As he pulled away she could tell from the look of wounded surprise in his eyes that he'd noticed her withdrawal.

'Emma? What's wrong?' he asked, his tone confirming his apprehension.

But before she could answer there was a long ring on the doorbell.

'That'll be Perdita,' Jack said, annoyance tingeing his voice. 'She's early.'

Jack paced the floor of the living room with a feeling of dread lying heavily in his gut while

Emma went to let Perdita and the photographer in.

He didn't understand why she was suddenly acting so coldly towards him after what they'd shared last night. The way she'd flinched away from his kiss had completely rattled him.

A moment later she reappeared with Perdita hot on her heels, the journalist bringing with her a cloud of the same cloying perfume she'd worn the last time they'd seen her.

Jack's stomach rolled as it twisted up his nose.

'Jack, darling! How lovely to see you again!' Perdita shot him a quick smile before striding around the room, glancing around at the décor that Emma had so painstakingly instated.

'What a wonderful room! The lighting is perfect for taking some photos of the two of you in here. What do you think, David?'

David, the photographer, nodded his agreement, then carelessly dumped his camera bag and laptop onto the polished cherry-wood coffee table.

Jack saw Emma wince in his peripheral vision, but she didn't utter a word of reproach. Perhaps she thought she had no right to because this wasn't her house. The thought frustrated him, making his limbs twitchy and his head throb.

'It's good for me,' David said, nodding at a light metre he was now holding up. 'I'll get set up while you do the interview, Perdie.'

'Okey-dokey,' Perdita trilled, turning to Jack with a simpering smile, then looking towards where Emma still stood in the doorway. 'Let's get started, shall we?'

They all sat down, he and Emma on the sofa next to each other and Perdita in the armchair opposite.

As Jack sat back his leg pressed up against Emma's and he bristled as she shifted away from his touch. Perdita was never going to believe they were a happily married couple if it looked as if she couldn't even stand to sit next to him.

What was going on? Had he done or said

something last night that had upset her? If he had, he had no idea what it could have been.

He took a breath and slung his arm around her shoulders. She tensed a little under his touch, but at least she didn't move away this time.

Looking over at Perdita, he steeled himself for spending the next half an hour—that was all he was going to give her—fielding her impertinent questions about his and Emma's life together, while also trying to make their relationship sound real and exciting enough to titillate the readers of *Babbler* magazine.

'So, how are the plans for the renewal of your wedding vows going?' Perdita purred, after she'd set up her phone to record their conversation.

'Er…well, we're still talking about when and how we're going to do it—' Emma said quickly, her smile looking fixed and her eyes overly bright when he glanced round at her.

'Uh-huh,' Perdita intoned, looking between the two of them with a quizzical little pinch in her forehead.

'We're hoping it'll be some time in the new year. We'll let you know when we've made some firm plans,' Jack said brusquely, in an attempt to close that line of questioning down as quickly as possible. Emma shuffled in her seat beside him.

Luckily Perdita didn't press them on it.

'So are you planning on spending Christmas here? I see you already have your decorations up,' Perdita said brightly, sweeping her hands around to gesture at the strings of silver baubles that Emma had hung from the picture rails and the spicy scented Douglas fir she'd covered with tasteful vintage Victorian ornaments.

'Yes, I think we'll be here for Christmas this year,' Jack replied, glancing around him at the decorations. They lent the room such a cosy festive air, so much so he found he was actually enjoying sitting in his living room for once, despite having to answer Perdita's inane questions.

'It must be so lovely to have a family home again to spend Christmas Day in, Emma. I understand you had to sell the house you grew up in after your poor father passed on,' Perdita cooed, raising her brow in a shocking show of pseudo sympathy.

'That's right, Perdita, we did,' Emma answered, keeping her chin up and her gaze locked with the woman's though Jack was aware of her shoulders tensing ever so slightly. 'And yes, it'll be a lovely house to spend Christmas in.'

He was desperate to call a halt to this ridiculous debacle, but he didn't want to give the woman the satisfaction of seeing him riled.

'You know, Perdita, Emma did all the interior design in the house,' he said, leaning in to draw the journalist's unscrupulous attention away from his wife.

Perdita glanced around at him, quickly hiding a flash of irritation that he'd foiled her underhand pursuit of some juicy gossip with which to titillate her readers. 'Is that right?'

'Yes. She has a real talent for it, my wife. I'm incredibly proud of her. In fact, why don't you mention to your readers that she's available for consultation if they're looking for an interior designer? I can give them a personal guarantee that they'll be delighted with Emma's talent for making a house into a home.'

He picked up Emma's hand from her lap, giving it a reassuring squeeze. After a second's pause she gave him a squeeze back.

There was definitely something very wrong here. Was she feeling ill? Too tired from their night of passion to think straight? Just sick to death of being hounded for answers to questions that brought up painful memories from her past?

Perdita continued to fire tricky questions at them: about how they fell in love, how they came to be reconciled, what their plans were for their future together and even though Emma fielded the questions well with vague but upbeat answers he imagined he could feel her slipping further and further away from him with every second that passed.

By the time the interview finally concluded

he was desperate to get Perdita out of the house so that he and Emma could talk again in private.

But unfortunately the journalist had other ideas.

'Well, I've got everything I need for the article. We just need to get some lovely snaps of the two of you together in this beautiful living room. You've done such a wonderful job on the décor, Emma. It'll make a lovely backdrop.'

She stood up from the armchair that she'd been perched on and Jack and Emma stood up awkwardly too.

Judging by the look on Emma's face, Jack was pretty sure she was as desperate for this to be over as he was.

'Are you ready for us, David?' Perdita called out to her photographer.

'As I'll ever be, Perdie,' David replied, shooting them all a wink.

They allowed Perdita to manhandle them into a 'loving' clinch on the sofa by the window, and

Jack's spirits sank even lower as he felt Emma tense as he wrapped his arms around her.

'Okay, let's have a lovely kiss now, shall we?' Perdita purred, giving them a lascivious smile.

To his horror, he realised Emma was actually vibrating with tension now and when he turned his head to look at her, his gut twisted as he saw only a cool remoteness in her eyes.

Leaning forwards, he pressed his lips to hers, hoping he could somehow wake the Emma from last night, to remind her how good it had been between them, and how good it could be again, if only she'd let him back in.

Her mouth was cool and pliant beneath his, but he could feel the reluctance in her, taste it on her lips, sense it in the raggedness of her breathing—as if she was only tolerating his touch until she could get away from him without looking bad in front of Perdita.

The rejection tugged hard at him, causing pain in his chest as if she'd torn something loose inside him.

'Wonderful!' Perdita said, as they drew apart.

'Is that it?' Jack asked gruffly, at the very end of his patience with the woman now. He wanted her and her nauseating presence out of his house so he could be on his own with Emma again and finally be able to find out what was going on with her.

'We're done,' Perdita said, all businesslike now as David gathered up his equipment behind her.

'I'll let your mother know when to expect to see the article,' she said.

As soon as he shut the door on Perdita's designer-suited back, Jack returned to the living room to find Emma perched on the arm of the sofa, staring out of the window.

'Thank you for doing that,' he said, walking towards her. 'I'm sorry to put you through it.'

She shrugged, but didn't look at him.

'I guess it'll satisfy your parents. At least for a while.' She took a deep shaky-sounding breath. 'I'm going to go now, Jack,' she said quietly, still not turning around.

His heart turned over at her words. 'What are you talking about?'

She turned to face him, her expression shuttered. 'I need to get out of here.'

Emma took a deep breath, trying not to let Jack's incredulous glare stop her from saying what needed to be said.

'I don't need to stay here now the journalists have stopped prowling around the house and Perdita's got her pound of flesh from us,' she said, keeping her voice steady and emotionless, even though it nearly killed her to do it.

Jack stared at her in shock. 'But you don't need to go, Em. You should stay. I want you to.'

She shook her head. 'I can't stay here now, Jack, not now we've crossed an irreversible line by sleeping together, something we agreed not to do.'

Couldn't he see that they shouldn't risk putting themselves in a position where it might happen again, that it would only make things harder and more complicated later when they started the inevitable divorce proceedings?

'I thought it's what you wanted too,' he ground out, his troubled gaze boring into hers. 'It certainly seemed like it last night.'

She folded her arms across her chest, hugging them around her. 'You didn't really think that one night together would fix what's wrong with our relationship, did you?'

His steady gaze continued to bore into hers, his eyes dark with intent. Sitting down opposite her, he put his elbows on his knees and leaned forwards, his eyes not leaving hers. 'Emma, I want us to try and make this marriage work.'

Her mouth was suddenly so dry she found it hard to swallow and she was aware of a low level of panic beginning to grow in the pit of her stomach.

'We've been apart for too long, Jack. How can we expect to make a relationship work now?' Her voice shook with the effort of keeping her emotions at bay.

'But it does work, Emma, we proved that last night.'

'You didn't really think we could just pick up from where we left off, did you?'

He blinked at her in surprise, then opened his mouth as if to answer.

But she couldn't let him try and persuade her otherwise; this was hard enough as it was. She really couldn't bring herself to trust that it could all be okay with them this time. What guarantees did they have that it wouldn't all fall apart again?

'We shouldn't have let last night happen. Sex always messes things up,' she said, her voice wobbling with tension.

He cleared his throat uncomfortably. 'Are you telling me you regret what happened now?' A muscle was twitching in his jaw and his brow pinched into a disbelieving frown.

She was hurting him; she could see it in his eyes and it was tearing her apart.

'I—can't do this again, Jack.' But her voice

held no conviction. She could see that he thought so too by the way he was looking at her.

As if he knew how very close she was to giving in.

He was still looking at her that way as he got up and walked towards her. Still looking as he pushed his hand gently into her hair and tilted her face towards him. Still looking as he brushed his lips against hers with a feather-light kiss that made her insides melt and fizz.

'Don't, Jack…' she murmured against his mouth, her willpower a frail and insubstantial thing that she was having trouble holding onto.

To her surprise he drew back, giving her the space she needed.

Finally acting as though he was *listening* to her.

Sliding his hand out of her hair, he took a deliberate step backwards, but didn't stop looking at her.

She felt the loss of his touch so keenly her body gave a throb of anguish.

'I want us to have another try at our marriage.' He took a breath. 'I need you.'

The passion and the absolute certainty she heard in his voice sent her heart into a slow dive, but she fought the feeling, still too afraid to believe what he was saying was true. 'You don't *need* me, Jack.'

'Yes, I do! There's this big hole in my life without you that I've never been able to fill. It's like part of me is hollow. A wound that just won't heal.'

'You're comparing me to a wound now? How romantic.' But despite her jibe she was aware of a warm glow of longing pulsing deep in her chest now.

She pushed it away, telling herself not to be a fool. It was dangerous to hope for this to work out after last time. Too much time and pain and heartache had come between them since those happier days. He was being naïve to think they could get back what they once had.

He locked his gaze with hers, his expression sincere. 'I'm going to be here for you this time,

Em, every step of the way. I'll look after you, I promise.'

'Promises aren't enough, Jack.'

He ran a hand over his face, suddenly looking tired. 'Then what do you want from me? Tell me, Emma!'

'A divorce! Like we'd planned!' she shouted back in frustration.

He stared at her in shock. 'You want to get a divorce after what happened between us last night?'

'It was just sex, Jack. We were both a little tipsy and feeling lonely. It was inevitable, I suppose, after all the time we've been spending together. But it didn't mean anything to me.' She swallowed hard, forcing back a lash of anguish as he stared at her with pain in his eyes.

'Don't tell me last night didn't mean anything to you because I won't believe you, Emma. You're not that good an actress,' he shot at her.

She recoiled at the fury in his voice, resentment suddenly rising from the pit of her belly at the unfairness of it all. 'You want to bet?' she retorted in anger. 'I've had years to perfect my mask. Years of smiling and looking serene in the face of some very taxing situations.'

'Is that what our marriage is to you? A *taxing situation*?'

'It hasn't been a marriage for years, Jack, just an inconvenience,' she shouted in utter frustration, feeling a jab of shame at how cruel that sounded.

Unable to bear the look of hurt on his face any longer, she strode away from him, banging her shin hard on the coffee table in her haste. But she didn't stop to soothe the pain away. She had to get out of there. Away from his befuddling presence. He was making her crazy—bringing back all these feelings she didn't want to have again.

'Where are you going?' he said, trying to block her path with his body, but she pushed past him, dodging away from his outstretched hand.

'Emma, can we please talk some more about this?'

'It's not what I want, Jack. I've already explained that. There's no point trying to hold onto the past. We can never get back what we once had. Everything's different now.'

'It doesn't have to be, Em. Fundamentally we're still the same people. We can make this marriage work.'

Shaking her head, she backed away from him. 'No, I'm sorry, Jack.' She took a deep shaky breath and dug her nails into her palms. 'I don't want to be married to you any more.'

Jack felt as though his heart were being crushed in his chest.

'Don't leave, Emma. Please. Stay and we'll talk some more about it.' He put a hand on her arm, aware that he was vibrating with fear now. *'Please.'*

Shaking her head, she pulled away from his touch and stumbled backwards. 'I can't, Jack.'

Her gaze met his and all he saw there was a wild determination to get away from him.

Chest tight with sorrow, he tried one last time to get through to her. 'Emma, I love you, please don't leave me again.'

Putting up a hand as if to block his words, she took another step away, reinforcing the barrier between them, rebuffing his pleas.

'I have to go,' she said, her voice rough and broken. 'I can't be here any more. Don't follow me. I don't want you to.'

And with that, she turned on her heel and strode away from him.

Frozen with frustration, he remained standing where she'd left him, listening to her mount the stairs and a minute later come back down, hoping—praying—that she'd pause on her way out, to stop and look at him one last time. If she did that, he'd go to her. Hold and comfort her. Tell her she could trust him and he'd make everything okay.

If she did that, he'd know there was still a chance for them.

But she didn't.

Instead he saw a flash of colour as she walked quickly past the doorway to the living room, and a few seconds later he heard the front door open, then close with the resounding sound of her leaving.

Silence echoed around the room, taunting him, widening the hollow cavity that she'd punched into his chest with her words.

Picking up a vase that Emma had bought as part of the house redecoration project, he hurled it against the wall with all his strength, drawing a crude satisfaction from seeing it smash into tiny little pieces and litter the floor.

He knew then that this was why he hadn't been back to see her in the six years since he moved to America. His heart had been so eviscerated the first time he hadn't wanted to risk damaging it again.

But the moment he'd seen her again at Fitzherbert's party he'd known in the deepest darkest recesses of his brain that he had to have her back. She was the only woman he'd ever loved and making himself vulnerable again for her would be worth the risk.

But it had all been for nothing.

Six years after she'd first broken his heart she'd done it to him all over again.

CHAPTER TEN

EMMA GOT OFF the plane in Bergerac, head-weary and heart-sore.

The very moment she saw her mother's anxious face in the crowd of people waiting to pick up the new arrivals at the airport, the swell of emotion that she'd been keeping firmly tamped down throughout the journey finally broke through. Tears flowed freely down her face as she ran into her mother's arms and held onto her tightly, burying her face in the soft wool of her jumper and breathing in her comforting scent.

'Darling, darling! What's wrong? I was so worried when I picked up your message. Is everything okay?' her mother muttered into her hair.

It took the whole of the thirty-minute journey to her mother's house in the tiny village of

Sainte-Alvère for Emma to explain—in a halting monologue broken with tears—about the marriage and aborted elopement and all that had happened to her since Jack had made his shocking reappearance.

Her mother listened in silence. Only once Emma had finished did she reach out her hand to cover her daughter's in a show of understanding and solidarity.

It was such a relief to finally talk to her mother about it all. She apologised profusely for keeping her in the dark for all this time, but, in a surprising show of self-awareness, her mother seemed more concerned with apologising to Emma for not being there to support her through such tough times.

A little while later they were ensconced on her mother's plant-pot-filled terrace sitting under thick woollen blankets, looking out over the fields behind the house with steaming cups of coffee cradled in their hands.

Philippe, her stepfather, had taken one look at her tear-stained face and promptly left the house so that she and her mother could talk on their own.

'Poor, Philippe, I hope he doesn't feel like I've chased him out of his own home,' Emma said, grimacing at her mother. 'He must still be in pain with his leg.'

'Don't be silly,' her mother said, flapping a hand. 'It's good for him to get out after being stuck here with just me for company for the last few days. He'll be much happier at the bar with Jean.'

Emma stared into the distance, watching the birds wheel in dizzying circles over a copse of trees as dusk fell, bathing the autumnal land-scape in a soft, hazy glow.

'You know, I keep asking myself why Jack would want to be with a lowly waitress when he's a billionaire earl,' she said quietly, turning to flash her mother a crooked smile.

Her mother frowned and swatted her hand dismissively. 'He won't be with a *waitress*, he'll be with *you*,' she said fiercely. 'What you do for a living has no bearing whatsoever on you as a person. I'm sure he'll tell you the same.'

Emma sighed and pulled the blanket tighter around her. 'Yeah, I know that really. It's just—' She paused, then said in a rush, 'What if it all went wrong again?'

Her mother smiled sadly. 'That's the chance you take when you fall in love. It's terrifying to make yourself vulnerable like that, but you know what? I was more afraid of what would happen to me if I didn't allow myself to have a relationship with Philippe. It was a good instinct to trust in his love because he brought me alive again.'

She watched her mother smooth her hands over the blanket on her lap.

'I still had to take a leap of faith when he asked me to marry him though,' her mother said, glancing at her with a small frown.

Emma tried to smile, but the muscles around her mouth refused to work, so she stared down at her hands in her lap instead, trying to get herself under control.

'Imagine the alternative, Emma,' her mother said, obviously noticing her distress. 'Imagine what you'll lose if you turn him away because you've given in to your fear. Imagine how that will make you feel. It'll eat away at you, darling—the "What if?"'

When she looked up she was surprised to see tears in her mother's eyes.

'This is all my fault. I should have been stronger for you when your father passed away, Emma. You were too young to take on all that responsibility by yourself—you were just a baby.'

Emma frowned. 'You weren't well, Mum. It wasn't your fault.'

Her mother shook her head, her bottom lip trembling. Lifting a hand, she touched her fingers softly to Emma's cheek. 'You lost your youth and innocence too early and look what it's done to you. You can't even let yourself be loved by a man who's perfect for you. You should. Give him a chance to prove himself to you, Emma. You owe him that much at least. You owe it to yourself to be happy.'

The memory of the hurt on Jack's face suddenly flashed across her vision, causing the hollow ache in her chest to throb and intensify.

Poor Jack.

He'd opened his heart to her and she'd pushed him away.

Again.

It had to have been just as hard for him to let himself fall in love with her again after the way she'd let him down, but he'd trusted his heart to her anyway, making the ultimate sacrifice.

Could she really not do the same for him?

Taking a long, deep breath, she felt determination start to course through her veins.

After everything she'd been through, was she really going to deny herself the chance to carve out a happy and rewarding life for herself?

In that moment she knew deep down that she wanted to be with Jack, she loved him and it was worth risking her heart if it meant she got the chance to be with him again.

But would Jack still want her after all she'd put him through?

There was only one way to find out.

She was going to have to go home and ask him.

His house, which had come alive with the addition of Emma's vibrant presence, felt still and vacant without her.

Lying awake until the early hours, tossing and turning in his empty bed, Jack relived the way Emma had rebuffed his affection with such vehement dismissal over and over again.

His stomach ached with misery as he finally gave up on sleep and made his way to his office at three in the morning.

He spent the rest of the early hours working on a project that had taken second place in his attention ever since Emma had reappeared in his life. Keeping busy had helped him the last time she'd left him, for a while at least, but it didn't seem to hold the same restorative powers any more.

Where was his wife?

He pictured her sleeping on one of her friends' sofas, getting on with her life without him. Going back to work for some idiot like Fitzherbert again. Keeping him well and truly out of the picture, only to turn up one day with divorce papers in her hands.

Finally, giving up on the hope of concentrating on anything else, he went to lie on the sofa and put the television on, staring at the news channel with unseeing eyes until exhaustion finally overtook him and dragged him into a restless sleep.

He woke a few hours later with a start, blearily checking his phone to realise with a shock that it was lunchtime.

Pulling himself into a sitting position, he was just about to haul himself up and go and make some strong coffee in the kitchen when a movement in the corner of his eye made him start in surprise.

Jumping to his feet, he turned to see Emma

standing in the doorway, looking at him with a hesitant smile.

'You came back,' was all he could utter past the huge lump in his throat, the unexpected sight of her standing there in front of him making him stupid with relief.

She walked tentatively into the room towards him, as if she wasn't sure what sort of reaction to expect. 'I'm so sorry I left, Jack.' She visibly swallowed. 'I was scared. Terrified to let myself love you again.' Breaking eye contact, she turned to glance out of the window, and let out a low laugh. 'Not that I ever really stopped.'

He stared at her, not sure whether to believe what he was hearing in case his addled brain was playing cruel tricks on him.

'Are you okay?' she asked shakily, turning back, her nose wrinkled with worry.

He continued to stare at her, only becoming aware that he was frowning when he noticed the anxiety in her expression.

Finally managing to pull himself together, he walked to meet her in the middle of the room and raised his hand to touch her soft cheek with his fingertips.

'Are you really here?' he murmured.

She laughed quietly and he saw relief in her face. 'It looks like I woke you. Did you sleep on the sofa all night?' she asked, her eyes clouding with concern.

He glanced back towards the rumpled cushions. 'Er...no. I couldn't sleep so I got up and worked, then I dozed off in here this morning.' He shook his head, trying to clear it. 'Where did you go?'

'To France. To see my mother.'

He nodded. 'Did you tell her about us?'

She smiled sheepishly. 'I did. She was really supportive. She basically told me to stop being such an idiot and to come back to the man I love.'

Emma couldn't help but smile at the almost comical look of relief on Jack's face.

'I guess I owe you an explanation about what

got me so spooked,' she said, waiting until he'd nodded before continuing.

She played with a loose thread on the sleeve of her jumper, summoning the courage to speak.

'I think losing you and my father in such quick succession must have damaged me on a fundamental level.'

She rubbed a hand over her face, letting out a low sigh.

'Ever since then I've been terrified of putting myself in a position where I have to trust my heart to someone again.'

He looked down at her with a small pinch between his brows. 'I understand that, Emma. It makes total sense after everything you've been through.'

'When it looked like it might be possible to have you again I panicked,' she said with a sad smile. 'I wanted you so much it scared me. I think I was afraid to be happy in case it was all whipped away from me again.'

She took a deep shaky breath.

'You know, the day we got married I couldn't

quite believe I could be so lucky as to have you. You were everything I'd ever wanted and when I looked at you I could see a bright shiny future shimmering in front of me. And then when it was whisked away from under my nose I sincerely wondered whether I was being punished for something. Up till then I'd led such a charmed life and just taken and taken without appreciating how much I had. Perhaps I was being penalised for my selfishness?'

'You weren't being selfish, you were living the life you'd been dealt and what happened was just really bad luck. It wasn't your fault. None of it was your fault.'

He sighed and frowned down at the floor, then looked up at her again with one eyebrow cocked.

'Pretending we were happily reconciled to everyone was a ridiculous thing to put ourselves through,' he said with a sigh. 'We should have been braver and talked about how we really felt, honestly and openly, instead of hiding and pretending there wasn't anything between us any more.'

He ran a hand through his hair, then scrubbed it across his face.

'I don't know what I was thinking, imagining I could have you living here, so close, without it driving me crazy with longing for you.'

Reaching out for her, he slid his hands around her waist and drew her nearer to him.

'Let's make a pact to deal with anything that comes at us *together* from this point on. We can take things as slowly as you like—take time to get to know each other properly again. I'm more than prepared to do that, Em. I just want you back in my life.'

There was a heavy beat of silence where they stared into each other's eyes.

'I love you, Emma,' Jack murmured.

She smiled as joy flooded through her. 'You really still love me after what I've just put you through?'

'Are you kidding? I've never *not* loved you.'

He gave her a squeeze. 'I'm in awe of you and

what you've achieved on your own—what you must have gone through to pay off those debts and what you've given up to do that. A lesser person would have thrown in the towel a long time ago. But you didn't and I have the utmost respect for you for that.'

She cupped his jaw in her hands, feeling his unshaven bristles tickling her palms. 'Thank you for saying that. It means a lot.'

She felt his chin slide beneath her touch as he turned his head until his lips came into contact with her palm. He kissed her there lightly, before turning back to look at her again.

'You know I'll support you in whatever you want to do, don't you?'

She flashed him a smile, excitement making her heart race. 'Actually, I've been wondering about training to be an interior designer. I'd have to go to college and become qualified for it, but I think it's something I'd love to do for a living.'

He nodded. 'If that's what you want I'll support you one hundred per cent with it. You can practise on this place if you like. As you've seen, it needs a lot more tender loving care upstairs, so perhaps you could fix the rest of it up as a practice project.'

'I would love that,' she said, a surge of joy lifting her onto her toes to kiss him.

His mouth was warm and firm and she sighed with relief as she felt his lips open under hers. And then he was kissing her fiercely, as if he never wanted to stop.

It felt so right, so absolutely *right* that it dragged all the breath from her lungs and the blood from her head, sending her dizzy with happiness. She knew with absolute certainty now that this was exactly where she was meant to be—in Jack's arms.

Finally, he drew away from her and she almost complained bitterly about the loss of his mouth on hers, until he pulled her tightly against his chest and held her there, safe in his embrace while they swayed gently together on the spot.

They stayed like that for a long time, feeling the beat of each other's hearts under their palms and listening to the gentle exhalation of their breath.

She knew then that she was never going to walk away from this man ever again.

On a sigh of satisfaction, Jack finally drew back and brought both hands up to cup her chin, gazing down into her eyes. 'I love you, Emma Westwood.'

Looking up into his handsome face, a face she knew as well as her own, she smiled at him with everything she had. 'I love you too.'

This admission seemed to galvanise something in him. Releasing his hold on her, he got down on one knee and looked up at her with resolution in his eyes.

'Well, in that case, will you renew your marriage vows with me?'

She looked down at the man she loved—had always loved—and knew in her heart that remaining married to him, fighting any battles she might encounter in the future with him there at her side, would make her the happiest woman on earth.

'I will!'

A wide smile of relief broke over Jack's face and he stood up and lifted her off the ground, hugging her fiercely to him.

'It looks like we've got another job to do, then—planning our vow renewal ceremony, which apparently is happening some time in the new year,' he said, pulling back to grin at her. 'Do you know anyone that can help us out with that?'

Emma smiled, imagining the looks of delight on Sophie, Grace and Ashleigh's faces when she asked for their assistance.

'I know exactly the right people to ask,' she said, bouncing up and down on the spot in her excitement. 'I can't wait to tell the girls our news. They're going to be thrilled!'

Jack smiled at her, his face alive with happiness, then drew her towards him, pressing his mouth to hers and sealing their future with a kiss to end all kisses.

* * * * *

MILLS & BOON®
Large Print – February 2017

The Return of the Di Sione Wife
Caitlin Crews

Baby of His Revenge
Jennie Lucas

The Spaniard's Pregnant Bride
Maisey Yates

A Cinderella for the Greek
Julia James

Married for the Tycoon's Empire
Abby Green

Indebted to Moreno
Kate Walker

A Deal with Alejandro
Maya Blake

A Mistletoe Kiss with the Boss
Susan Meier

A Countess for Christmas
Christy McKellen

Her Festive Baby Bombshell
Jennifer Faye

The Unexpected Holiday Gift
Sophie Pembroke

MILLS & BOON®
Large Print – March 2017

Di Sione's Virgin Mistress
Sharon Kendrick

Snowbound with His Innocent Temptation
Cathy Williams

The Italian's Christmas Child
Lynne Graham

A Diamond for Del Rio's Housekeeper
Susan Stephens

Claiming His Christmas Consequence
Michelle Smart

One Night with Gael
Maya Blake

Married for the Italian's Heir
Rachael Thomas

Christmas Baby for the Princess
Barbara Wallace

Greek Tycoon's Mistletoe Proposal
Kandy Shepherd

The Billionaire's Prize
Rebecca Winters

The Earl's Snow-Kissed Proposal
Nina Milne